The Concubine and Her Vampires

First Edition May 2018

ISBN: 978-1-77357-053-2,

978-1-77357-052-5

Legal File Usage – Your Rights

Table of Contents

Dedication

To Gina for finding the story inside me.
You knew it was there. Love you.

To Heather and Brittany. Thank you for
being with me on this wild ride!

"A lady's imagination is very rapid; it jumps from admiration to love, from love to matrimony in a moment."

— Jane Austen, Pride and Prejudice

"Imagination is like a muscle. I found out that the more I wrote, the bigger it got."

— Philip José Farmer

About The Concubine and Her Vampires

When destiny becomes reality...

Born a blood demon, Olivia Martin's sole purpose is to become a blood slave to a vampire. She is nothing more than a blood bag.

With a vampire as her master, she would want for nothing, her every need and whim catered to, but becoming a prisoner was not the life Olivia would have chosen for herself.

At least, until she met Jared and his four brothers-at-arms. Giving yourself to one person was easy. Having fun with two, exciting. But a harem of lovers? It was more than Olivia ever considered possible. Need, lust, and blood drive Olivia to find a strength inside herself to not only accept her five sexy-as-sin vampires, but to also protect herself from an evil hell bent on claiming her for its own.

The Concubine

and

Her Vampires

A Paranormal Reverse Harem Novel

Julie Morgan

Naughty Nights Press • Canada

Chapter One

THE SUN FADED in the distance over New Orleans, leaving pink and orange highlights across the sky. The air was humid and thick. Olivia Martin rubbed the inside of her forearm. A birthmark that had been faint her entire life, until last month, turned darker, and became more prominent. She pulled up her sleeve and glanced down at the blemish.

The mark, a circular shape, similar to a maze, with five horn-like extensions.

She rubbed her hand over it, then crossed her arms over her chest. This may be the last time she watched a sunset. Once she went underground, she may only see the stars, the moon...

Born as a nephilim, she bore the mark identifying her as a blood demon. It was not something she asked for, but it was not a choice given to her, either. Her human mother had been seduced by an Incubus. At least, that's what she told Olivia. It wasn't the best bedtime story. Thankfully, it wasn't, 'Hey daughter of mine. I laid with a demon. Bam, that's how you were conceived.'

She knew of vampires, they existed in her world. Not everyone knew, but as a concubine it was her future, her destiny. Olivia wondered if this would ever shift her into becoming a succubus.

Could be worse ways to go, I suppose. Sex demon isn't so bad.

When she performed a Google search on Succubus demons, she shuddered. Wings with a long tail? No thanks.

This was her destiny and whether she was ready or not to embrace it, she needed to be prepared.

She sighed and turned back to her car. Tomorrow would be her final day as a human. Tomorrow night, she would be introduced to the coven as the concubine to her vampire. She would be arranged to suit a vampire's needs the rest of her natural life, or until he died, whichever came first. Once her fate had been sealed to said vampire, she would be tied to him, completely. It was not uncommon for the vampire and concubine to become mated pairs, however, if the vampire were already involved, fights had been known to happen. Not just fights, blood battles.

Vampires were much stronger, invincible to most things, as opposed to humans. If someone's mate challenged her for their vampire, she would not stand a chance. That was, of course, unless said vampire defended her, resulting in her vampire fighting against their own mate.

Talk about a blood battle.

She shuddered once more. No one had ever wanted her that much in her life. She had lovers but no one ever serious enough to propose marriage. Not that she could have accepted anyway.

Once Olivia was paired, she would be set for life, wanting for nothing. It wasn't a bad trade off. Not having a normal life, though, no husband, children, grandchildren...not that she wanted that right now, but if she had, the future of such aspect had been stripped of her at birth.

As a blood demon, she had no actual powers that a demon would possess, but rather she could ingest blood in place of food for sustenance. The thought made her stomach churn. She had only ever tasted blood when she'd bite the inside of her cheek or tongue. The iron taste was not something she ever desired. She read that would change once you were with your vampire. The taste would give a euphoric sensation. All of her senses would be heightened.

She recalled of her last boyfriend going down on her. He was okay but not sensational. He would be down there for what felt like hours with little real result. If he were a vampire, though, if the stories were true, she would not be able to control herself, or the orgasms she had. And there were fangs.

The thought of fangs scared her. Hell, needles frightened her. Once she was paired, fangs would be her life.

She drove home, making mental notes of her belongings. She arranged to have her clothes and personal effects brought to her new home. Once she knew where she would end up, directions would be given at that time. Parking in her driveway, she sighed and lifted her gaze to the front of her rental property. She would miss this house. She never bought property. Why would she? She would end up selling it to move.

Sliding out from behind the wheel, she pulled her purse over her shoulder, locked her car, and walked to her front door. She unlocked it and sauntered inside. Closing it behind her, she glanced through her mail and walked through her home to the kitchen. The light buttery walls lit her spirits, a welcoming color to the darkness of her world. She stopped on an envelope with a wax seal.

Do people still do this?

She did recognize it, though. It was the seal of the counsel, the vampire counsel. Breaking the seal with a nail, she opened the letter and pulled out a tanned invitation.

You are cordially welcomed to the introduction of concubine Olivia Martin...

She trailed off reading and sat the invitation on the counter. They sent her an invitation to her own ceremony. Why? So maybe she wouldn't forget to show up?

"Assholes," she mumbled. The meowing from her cat, Sherlock, caught her attention. Her midnight black cat stared up at her with his golden eyes. He meowed again. "Hungry?" she asked. As if Sherlock could answer, he meowed.

She laid out food for her feline friend and walked into her den. Taking a seat on her sofa, she turned on the television and stared at it. The news played, but she wasn't listening. Soon would be the ceremony, her pairing...vampires.

What vampire will request my hand in the pairing?

Will he be sexy?

Old, fat, and ugly?

Hell, maybe a woman?

She shook her head and tucked her legs up underneath her. Sherlock jumped up on the couch. She pulled him into her lap and stroked his head.

Vampires.

Feedings.

Concubine.

Mistress.

It was all too much to consider as her future. If she ran and refused this life, they would hunt her down. They left her no choice. This will be her life.

"Tomorrow, human woman Olivia Martin will voluntarily sacrifice herself for the greater good."

Olivia glanced to the television as the reporter continued, catching her attention.

"Her pairing will be a successful one, and she will make her coven proud." The reporter grinned.

Olivia blinked and rubbed her eyes. She stared at the television. The reporter droned on about who would be playing what sport, what crimes happened in the area, and the weather.

Was she daydreaming this? It's possible she was losing her mind and the pairing had not even started.

She laid down, resting her head on the shoulder of the couch. She curled up Sherlock next to her and he purred. Exhaustion set in, as well as depression. Olivia wanted to love someone and be loved in return. She wanted to make love going to bed and wake up to her man giving her oral sex. She wanted to wrap herself in saran wrap as a welcome home surprise. No man she had dated before wanted that from her, though.

Olivia had curves, her body thick. She liked her figure and didn't care for men who wanted the stick thin women. That would never be her, and she was good with that. But when a man told her not to wear this, or don't dress like that, she'd let them go.

She wanted to have someone hold her during the rough days and laugh with her at silly movies. She just wanted a life of her own. She would never have it. A tear slipped into her hair.

She thought of her mother just then. Olivia had held on to the anger against her mother up until the day she passed away. The moments before she took her final breath, her mother had whispered, "Forgive me."

Her eyes burned, the memories bringing on a fresh set of tears. Olivia was alone in the world. Having a coven take care of her was not the worst thing in the world, but it wasn't the best, either.

She swiped her tears away and closed her eyes, allowing the upcoming events to continue their onslaught as she slipped into unconsciousness. Tomorrow would be the first day to the rest of her life.

Chapter Two

THE DAY HAD arrived, her day to become a concubine. Olivia was not thrilled. High-strung nerves made her stomach roll and bile claw its way up her throat. She brushed her teeth and ran her hairbrush through her hair. Soon, the beautification process would begin. Hairstylists, professional dressers, and a nail tech would arrive. The last time she did any kind of prep like this was her high school prom.

She glanced at her phone. They should be here in five minutes. She put her brush away and pressed her elbows to the vanity, her chin resting on her hands. Sucking in a deep breath, she exhaled and watched her reflection in the mirror. Her chestnut brown hair hung to her waist, soft curls giving it a slight wave. She closed her eyes and lowered her head. Then the doorbell rang.

"Fuck," Olivia whispered, then stood. She peeked into the mirror once more, then nodded. "Let's do this."

Making her way to the door, she saw two women and one man dressed in black cloaks, faces and heads obscured with a hat and shawl similar to a bee keeper, and black gloves on their hands.

Vampires.

She opened her door and the trio quickly stepped inside. No introductions. Olivia closed the door and stared at her visitors.

"So, umm, hi. I'm Olivia." She waved one hand then wrapped her arms around her waist.

The women pulled the gloves off their hands, then removed their wide brimmed hats. They almost reminded her of the Preachers she saw occasionally with their Sunday hats going to Catholic mass. The one to her left unwrapped her shawl from her face. Her skin was alabaster, her eyes a light hue of blue. Her hair crimson, like fire. The corners of her mouth lifted in a grin.

"Hi there. My name is Amanda. I'll be doing your hair today."

Amanda had a southern drawl as apparent as Olivia's.

"I have Jackie next to me here," Amanda nodded to the other woman, then motioned to the man. "This here is Bryce. Jackie will do your nails. Bryce will dress you."

Bryce removed his hat and shawl. "We're going to make you look like you walked off the Hollywood carpet." His voice was heavy, gravelly. The shirt covering his body was taut around his thick arms. The pectorals on his chest twitched when he moved his arms. Hell, he was built like a lumberjack. His skin was pale, like Amanda's, but with dark hair and light tan eyes, like coffee mixed with cream. He smirked. "You will walk in and look like the princess you are."

Olivia lifted her brow. "I'm no princess, but I don't mind looking pretty." She flashed a glance at Jackie. The woman had blonde hair and sapphire eyes, like the ocean near the Caribbean.

Like Amanda.

The vampire curled her fingers, motioning Olivia to come to her. She stepped toward her and Jackie grasped her hand.

She tilted her head at Olivia's nails. "Not bad, but I'll make them better."

"Right," Olivia said and freed her hand from Jackie's. "What do you need me to do?"

***

The team brought in their supplies, consisting of hair products, curling irons, makeup, and clothes. Lots and lots of clothes.

An hour had passed but to Olivia it felt like it was only minutes. She wanted the time to draw out. The longer the process took, the better. When she was done, she would be escorted to the coven.

"Are you excited?" Amanda asked.

"I'm not sure, honestly," Olivia told her.

"You've known about this your whole life. Aren't you curious?"

"Well, yes, I am, but I'm not sure what to expect. I don't know how I fit in, other than being a feeding source." She lifted her hands up to stop Amanda, then turned in her seat. "May I ask you something?"

Amanda nodded with a smile. "Of course."

"Does it hurt?"

"Does what hurt, hun?"

Olivia cleared her throat. She did not want to offend the woman but had many questions she could not ask just anyone. She tried again. "Amanda, when I'm bitten, will it hurt?"

Amanda shook her head. "Not in the least. You will feel nothing of the sort. You will feel something," she giggled, then continued, "but it won't be pain."

Olivia lifted her brows then felt blood rush to her cheeks. She lowered her gaze to the floor. "Well, that's good to know."

Amanda touched Olivia's chin with a finger and tilted her head up, forcing Olivia to meet her gaze. "No one will force you into something you don't want to do. If you permit feeding only, then that is all it will be. If you allow more to happen, like sex, then it will, but only by your permission. No one takes a concubine against their will."

Olivia nodded. "Thank you," she whispered, turning back around in her seat. "Any idea who I'm promised to?"

Amanda shrugged. "I have an idea, but the surprise is best when you don't know. Now, then." She pulled the top part of Olivia's hair back and pinned it. "You're stunning." She walked around to face her and picked up her makeup bag.

"Ready for me?" came a voice behind them. Olivia glanced in the mirror as Jackie entered the room.

"Yeah, go ahead. I'm almost done here," Amanda told her.

"You look divine, my love," Jackie boasted. "I'm going to shape your nails and paint them to match the lipstick you'll wear. I have a feeling Bryce will dress you in red tonight! You'll stand out, most certainly!"

Olivia beamed and allowed Jackie to take her hand. She felt like a celebrity being worked on. "I don't necessarily like to stand out. I'm more like paint on a wall. I would rather blend in and not be noticed."

"Oh, you're shy?" Jackie asked.

"I wouldn't call it being shy, but I'm quite introverted. I keep to myself."

"Well," Jackie started. "Other concubines will be at the coven. But once you're paired, you'll live with your vampire."

"Or vampires," Amanda added.

Olivia's stomach dropped. Did she hear her right? She stared Amanda, then turned to glance at Jackie, then back to Amanda. "Did you say vampires, plural?"

Mischief sparkled in the hairdresser's eyes. "It is up to you, but more the merrier, right?"

Olivia wanted to become one with the chair, right now, more than anything. She was the woman who liked sex with the lights off. She didn't like being ogled by anyone, definitely not a group of men. She swallowed past the lump that had formed in her throat. "Wh-wh—" she took a deep breath and tried again. "What's the likeliness of a multiple arrangement happening?"

Amanda came around to Olivia's front and squatted down. She grasped her hands and smiled. "My dear, as I said, nothing will happen without your consent. There is nothing to be scared of."

"Unless it's Victor," came Bryce's voice as he entered the room.

If looks could kill, Amanda would have burned Bryce right then with her death glare. "What the hell is wrong with you?"

Olivia pressed her lips together to keep herself from giggling. As much as she was not looking forward to this arrangement, she'd begun to grow fond of Amanda. "Who is Victor?"

"Only the richest, most powerful vampire," Bryce said. "He thinks his dick is the size of his bank account."

Olivia laughed out, then covered her lips. "Oh, I'm sorry."

"Don't be, "Amanda told her. "Victor thinks all things are his. You know, boy in a sandbox, all toys are his."

This alarmed Olivia. What if this Victor showed up tonight and had an interest in her? If he decided he wanted her, could he have the power to sway the ceremony? Would the elders allow it to happen?

"I know what you're thinking," Jackie offered and patted Olivia's hand. "He has no right or say so over anyone who comes in, or who they will be paired with. As much as he wants to rule and run things, he cannot."

A bit of the weight she felt lifted. "Well, that's good to know. I'm still curious about this entire pairing. What if the vampire does not find me attractive?"

Amanda pulled a few curls down to fall around Olivia's shoulders. "Once the pairing is done, looks do not matter. You will become his."

"What if the pairing is with a woman?"

"Do you prefer women?" Jackie asked.

Olivia shook her head. "No, but what about male concubines?"

"We have pairings that go both ways," Jackie told her. "And if we're not paired, well, there's volunteers we can feed from."

"You never want to be a volunteer," Amanda whispered in her ear.

"Why not?" Olivia whispered back.

"If the vampire dies before their concubine, the human is kept at the coven. It would be impossible to live among humans with everything they have learned about our kind. As a concubine, once you have tasted and experienced vampire blood, it becomes something of an addiction. If you're not paired, or refuse everyone presented, and opt to become a volunteer, you, well, for lack of better words, become a blood whore. The addiction is demanding and will consume your life."

Olivia considered this for a moment. If her vampire died, she could not leave. If she were to run away, they would find her and bring her back. She would have to be the one who died to escape this reality. She closed her eyes and let out a deflated breath.

"Olivia," Jackie whispered. "Please, trust me. The vampire you will be paired with, he will treat you well. You will be precious to him."

"I will be his blood bag. How is that precious?" She asked and opened her eyes.

Jackie smiled to Olivia. "I promise, you'll see. Look, I'm all done." She stood and put the nail polish down. "I only need to do your toes, which will take a minute."

Olivia looked at herself in the mirror. Her hair was styled, makeup perfect. She shifted her gaze to her hands. She felt like a prisoner inside the body of a celebrity. It was not fair. None of this was.

"So, I see it is now my turn?" Bryce asked.

Leaning in the doorjamb of her bedroom, Bryce winked at her. She smiled at the man. She couldn't help it. As rugged and outdoorsy as Bryce appeared to be, he exuded excitement like a kid in the candy store.

"I wish I could wear these," he teased with a wink. "But I don't think they make my size."

Olivia giggled and stood. She followed Bryce to her bedroom. Her queen-sized bed had clothes set out over the entire thing. She could not see any of the pillows. Her artwork on the wall became hangers for dresses. Her mirror was covered with a shawl.

"How am I supposed to see myself?" she asked.

"You won't," Bryce told her and motioned her further into the room. "You will only see yourself after this point in time once you're paired."

She frowned. "What for? I'd love to see my dress."

"Well, look down," he said. "Now, come on, take off your clothes."

She froze and stood silent, fear creeping up her spine. She shook her head.

"Olivia," Bryce whispered. "I prefer the cock to the pussycat. Don't worry, I think you have an amazing body."

Olivia laughed and side-glanced at Bryce. The man was grinning, and he shrugged. She really liked her dress team. Would they be around once she was with her vampire? She would have to find out.

Moments later, Bryce was pulling dresses over her head, zipping her up, shaking his head, undressing her, and starting anew. He was good, though. He never once messed with her hair. Amanda would most definitely follow through with the death glare and use a knife.

"Oh," Olivia began when a question hit her. "So, no sun?"

"Correct," Bryce answered. "Arms up, one more dress."

She lifted her arms. "Garlic?"

He chuckled. "Nope."

She nodded, then turned around once the dress was over her head. The coolness of the satin felt nice. The material was a bright hue of crimson, like a new red car. "Stakes to the heart?"

"It would definitely hurt from penetration, but no."

"Hmm," she pondered.

"Decapitation," he whispered.

"Oh." She turned to face him once she was zipped. "That's dreadful. And messy."

Bryce chuckled. "Yes, it is. And, Olivia, we have found the winner!" He clapped his hands under his chin and beamed with excitement. "Ladies, come check out our charge!"

Their charge, she wondered. She let it go. "So, doable?"

Amanda nodded.

Jackie gasped.

"You look amazing, Olivia. Simply divine! You will have all heads turning in your direction tonight," Jackie said. "Let me paint your toes and get them dry, then slip on your shoes!"

All heads in my direction?

No, thank you.

She'd keep to herself to avoid eye contact, if possible. Jackie tended to her feet then Bryce brought out a pair of low heels.

"Oh, that's not what I expected," Olivia said. "With the dress and the hair, I figured I would be in stilettos."

"I can make that happen, but honestly, Olivia, you'll thank me for this. The floor is concrete in the coven. It's chilly. You'll want to wear these shoes. I'll also provide you with a shawl."

She nodded. "Thank you for taking care of me today. Will I see you three after I've been paired?"

"It's possible," Amanda told her. "You may call on us anytime to come do your hair, nails, or dress you for an occasion."

"Will there be occasions for this?"

"Sure," Amanda said with a smile. "Tell your vampire you're lonely and want female companionship."

Bryce cleared his throat.

"If I need a personal shopper you'll be my top person," Olivia said to him.

Amanda took her hands and held Olivia's arms out. "Wow, you're a vision."

Olivia blushed and shifted her gaze to the floor.

"Try to keep eye contact with your vampire when he addresses you," Amanda offered. "It's respectful. He'll appreciate that."

She nodded. "Thank you. Anything else I should know?"

"Just try to enjoy yourself. You'll have everything you need at your fingertips," Jackie told her.

Olivia nodded once more. She lowered her arms to her side and turned away from her new friends. She was about to give up her life as a human to embark on a new journey as a concubine. She held her head up, pushed back her shoulders, and stood with feigned confidence as she turned to face her trio. "Let's go. I don't want to keep them waiting."

She hoped her false self-assurance masked the fear she felt. When she walked through the doors as a human, they would close behind her as a concubine. Her vampire would be a stranger, or worse, *vampires*. She picked up the handbag Bryce had matched with her dress, and followed her team toward the door. With a final glance at her home, she turned on her heel and walked outside.

The sun had set, and the stars twinkled in the sky. She shivered slightly. She felt a shawl cover her shoulders and she smiled. "Thank you, Bryce."

"You're welcome." He opened the back door to the dark stretch limo parked on her street. "Your chariot awaits, princess."

She walked the short length of her driveway, curious if her neighbors knew where she was headed, and if they knew they would never see her again. At this point, it did not matter. What mattered tonight was surviving the introduction as a concubine and leaving with her new paired partner.

Chapter Three

THEY SAY WHEN death approaches, your life comes in flashes, like an audiobook played on high speed. Others have said it's like walking the green mile.

Dead man walking, there's a dead man walking here. Get out of the way, dead man walking.

The limo drove just over the speed limit, or so Olivia considered by the way the city streaked by her window. When would she see the streets again? The lamp lights? The sun?

Oh damn, I'm going to miss the sun, so much.

She sighed and crossed her legs. If she wanted something new, she would have a personal shopper. Something made? Personal cook, or assistant, or whatever it was she desired. People longed to live this way. So many desire to want for nothing. Olivia thought this was what she wanted, until she realized what she had to give up in order to obtain it.

Nerves jolted in her belly when the limo turned a corner and then pulled to a stop.

"Miss Martin, we're here," called the driver. "Please, wait in your seat. Someone will come fetch you."

She lifted a brow. "What the fuck am I," she whispered. "A dog?" She thought she saw the driver smirk. She picked up her phone and checked the time. Nine pm. Nerves were now joined with impatience. She was here to meet her destiny, and destiny wanted her to wait.

She pulled her pocket mirror from her handbag and checked her lipstick and makeup. Everything still in its place. Nothing had smeared or needed touching up. Her team did an amazing job. Highlights, contours, all the new ways to do makeup, hair, and nails. They had it down perfect.

Bryce provided a few rings he told her were hers to keep, a gift from the coven. A pink diamond sat on her right ring finger, princess cut. It was set on a platinum mount. The ring was exquisite. A diamond bracelet rested on her wrist.

She felt as if she were being watched. She glanced up to the rearview mirror. The driver had been watching her. Their gazes met, and he quickly looked away. "How much longer will I remain in the car?"

"When they're ready to retrieve you, someone will be out," he answered.

Again, with the dog remarks.

"What's your name?"

"Theodore, but you may call me Ted."

"Nice to meet you, Ted. Are you the official driver for the coven?"

"Not quite," he told her.

"Oh, then who do you drive for?"

Before he could answer her, Ted turned his head in the direction of the building. "Your party comes. Nice to meet you, Olivia."

She tried to smile, but her heart dove into her stomach. She felt nauseous. The limo locks unlatched, and the door was opened. Night air blew into the car and a large hand with a midnight black sleeve reached in, palm up.

"Miss Martin?" called the deep, gravelly voice attached to the arm. "Please, join me."

She tucked her purse under her arm and slipped her hand into his. She stood from the car and the stranger holding onto her hand made sure she was upright before he released her. The man shut the door, then turned to her.

"My name is Jesse. I'm assigned as your detail."

She looked up to Jesse. The man was huge. He towered over her small size. She took a step back and lifted her brows.

"Nice to meet you, Jesse. Why would I need a detail?"

He smirked and offered his hand once more. She put hers in his and he tucked her hand into the crook of his elbow. "I'm to keep you safe until the pairing."

"Safe? Safe from what?"

"Not what," he answered. "From who."

Fear struck her, and she paused in her step. "Jesse, what will happen to me in there?"

"Nothing you don't want to happen, Miss Martin."

"Please, Olivia. And, if I don't want this?"

"Well, unfortunately, you're not able to get out of this. You're a blood demon. You were born to feed the coven."

She closed her eyes. "Then, why dress me up for a funeral?"

"Come again?" he asked.

"I feel like I'm walking toward my death."

Jesse turned to face her. "No one in there can force you into anything you do not want. Once you're inside and you see what all this is about, you'll understand, and will feel safe. I'll be by your side until the pairing. Once it's done, then I'll hand you off."

She nodded, but still did not like what she was about to walk into, safe or not.

"All right, let's do this."

Jesse escorted her to a set of double doors to what appeared to be a warehouse. She glanced up to Jesse and motioned to the building with her thumb. "Incognito?"

He nodded. "Not everyone can know where we are. Imagine humans finding out we're real, or you're real."

"But, I am real."

He smiled. "That's not what I meant."

"Thank you for being nice to me. I wasn't sure what to expect."

He bowed his head. "Are you ready?"

She nodded. "Yes."

Jesse opened a panel and punched in a set of codes. "So, you know what to expect, you're not the only concubine here."

"Oh? Is this some type of claiming ceremony?"

He nodded. "Something like that."

"Oh hell, I was only teasing."

The doors unlocked, and Jesse pulled one of them open. "Don't let go. You'll be fine next to me. Vampires will approach you and look you over. Speak when spoken to. Understand?"

Tears burned her eyes. She wanted to cry. She felt like a cow being sent in for slaughter. She nodded.

They stepped inside, and the doors closed, then locked. The area was small, like a passage between the outside and the event inside. A familiar sound of a fan motor hummed in the distance. She swallowed hard, her throat dry. Light classical music echoed from another room. They walked toward the source and her heels struck the concrete below her feet. Fear escalated further as they approached the next door.

Jesse pulled on the door and the music escaped and surrounded her. Inside, a chandelier hung overhead. The walls were red velvet with silver wall decor. The air felt chilly and she was grateful for the shawl Bryce provided her. She tugged the silver garment closer around her shoulders. The men were in tuxedos, women in beautiful dresses. First thing she noticed about this was the men were all in black. Some had bowties, others regular ties. Most of the women were also in black. Then, there were women in different colored dresses.

Those must be the concubines.

Jesse escorted her inside and stopped, just short of the dance floor. Just as her dress team stated, the men turned to gaze upon her. She felt exposed and vulnerable. Her knees shook, and she wanted to cry.

"Calm yourself," Jesse ordered. "You're digging your nails into my arm."

"I'm sorry," she whispered. "Everyone is staring."

He smirked and leaned down to her. "Imagine walking into an art gallery.

Amazing pieces of work hang on the walls, painted by world class artists. Each piece has a number assigned, like one fifty of four hundred. Then there is a painting brought into the room with no numbers. It is a one of a kind image that can be obtained by only one collector. Everyone wants this one of a kind. Olivia, you are that painting."

Her heart leapt in her chest. "No one has ever compared me to something so precious before in my life."

He lifted his brow. "Tonight will be interesting."

She frowned. "Was that supposed to be a joke?"

He chuckled. "Can I get you a drink?"

She nodded. "A shot of something fierce."

He nodded. "Water it is. Quiet now." He walked her to the bar and waved down the bartender. She continued to look over the people, taking all of this in.

She had known about blood demons, Incubus, Succubus, and vampires her entire life. People were smiling, laughing, drinking, enjoying conversation. She noticed a few would follow her every move, others went back to their conversations.

Jesse handed her a glass of clear liquid with ice cubes. She took it and smelled it. Satisfied it was water, she sipped it.

"I wouldn't give you something loaded."

She arched a brow.

"You may speak."

"I'm not a fan of not speaking. But, since I have permission now," she said and stepped closer to him. She didn't know the man, but right now, she felt his protection. "Tell me about the men who may try to pair with me."

"I'd rather you meet them before I say anything."

"What about Victor?"

Jesse snarled. He actually snarled. "Victor will do good to keep away from you."

She raised her brows. "He's that bad?"

"Let's just say he won't be given a pairing anytime soon."

"Why? What did he do?"

"That's a story for another time. Soon, the introductions will begin."

Olivia sipped her water and held onto Jesse. He guided her toward the center of the room, pointing out a few people in attendance, explaining that they had been with the coven for more than a century. The eldest vampire attending tonight's pairing has had four concubines. The oldest recorded vampire in history had fifteen.

Olivia could not imagine going through life having fifteen women spend their life with a man who would not love them, make children with them, marry them.

They keep telling me it'll change once the pairing happens. We'll see.

The music dwindled away after the last song finished. Anyone dancing left the dance floor. Everyone in black made their way toward the walls of the room, leaving the floor space open.

Jesse held onto her hand on his arm. He took a step forward, leading her ahead.

Olivia's breath became sparse. Her lungs burned and she couldn't breathe. She shook her head and tugged on Jesse.

"Please, don't make me do this," she whispered.

"I promise you will be safe. Now, please, behave."

She wanted to cry, run away, rip her heels off and use them as weapons.

A loud creek of hinges erupted in the silence as a set of wooden double doors opened in the shadowed back of the room. Someone coughed. Olivia's heart pumped loud in her ears and she vaguely wondered if anyone else could hear the thumping beat.

Heel strikes from men's shoes began to echo. Olivia waited and soon, shadows formed in the dimness of the room as they entered from the long hallway beyond the doors. One by one, elegantly dressed vampires filed out, walking the circumference of the room. A few made eye contact with Olivia. She wanted to look down, hide behind Jesse.

"Keep eye contact, don't look away. And don't speak—"

"Yes, got it," she interrupted. She felt him chuckle.

In all, twenty-five different men left the confines of the narrow hallway and the doors closed behind them. They trolled the floor, looking over each woman as though they intended to select the choicest morsel of meat from the offerings. Her eyes widened, her lips parting slightly as she drew in a deep breath. Each one of the vampires appeared to have just walked off a photoshoot. Holy hell, every single one of them were sexy as sin.

This may have been what Amanda and Jackie were talking about.

Two men stepped up to her. One with short, chestnut brown hair and striking hazel eyes. He tilted his head down and kept his gaze locked with hers. He did not move, blink, or make an attempt to speak to her.

Olivia held her breath. The man in front of her had to be the most attractive man she had ever seen. She wanted to tilt her head, exposeher neck for him to bite. As soon as the thought crossed her mind, fear crept back in and sent a chill skating down her spine.

Fangs.

Needles.

Vampires.

She felt her body shake with fear. The man before her took a step closer. He reached up and trailed a finger over her cheek. He leaned in and sniffed. He legitimately sniffed her. Then he leaned in closer and inhaled deeply. She could feel his nose tickle her neck.

Olivia closed her eyes. She had never had a stranger come this close to her, but at the same time, he calmed her.

"Remember to breathe, so you don't pass out," the man whispered to her.

He pulled back and met her gaze once more, then winked.

A smile crept over her lips as she relaxed.

"Who do we have here?" came a man behind her sniffer.

"Please," the man offered and stepped to the side.

A man, whom she assumed from his accent to be Italian, stepped forward. His dark hair was longer, to his shoulders, with soft curls. Olivia wanted to run her fingers through his hair. He was just as sexy, just as gorgeous, as the first man. He smiled and stepped closer, then leaned in. Like the former, he inhaled her scent.

What are they doing?

Why sniff me?

"Thank you," the man said and stepped back. "We're done here." Both men turned to head back to the inner part of the circle.

Olivia wanted to reach after them, ask them to come back. Something about them pulled to her, urged her to give herself to them. But why?

"Not so bad, right?" Jesse offered.

"What?" She asked and blinked.

He chuckled. "Nothing. You're doing fine. But, please, breathe."

She nodded and sucked in a deep breath, then turned back toward the men in the crowd. The two who had sniffed her were lost in the crowd. She felt sad. She attracted men, but never men like these two. Would she be paired to both men? One of them? Neither?

"Welcome to the formal introduction! Welcome to our new concubines!"

A man's voice bellowing out over a microphone startled Olivia. The group of men spread out across the floor and the two men came back into view. Olivia smiled.

She'd walked in feeling fearful and wanting to leave. Now, she wanted these two men to call on her for the pairing. She felt shallow for feeling this way, but every one of the men in the crowd were simply astonishing. She leaned into Jesse.

"Which one is Victor?"

Jesse looked across the crowd. "At your eleven o'clock. Hands are in his pockets. Dark hair."

She shook her head. "That explains over half of the men."

He chuckled. "Second from the end on the left."

Olivia peeked over to where Jesse mentioned, then gasped. The man was staring at her. He grinned and she saw his fangs. Fear crept inside her once more. She gripped Jesse again.

"Please, bring forth, concubine Melissa," the man with the microphone announced.

A woman in a light pink dress was guided forward by her escort. Three men stepped toward her, each of them sniffing her like the two had done to Olivia. The men then took a step back and whispered to each other. A moment later, two left and one stayed. He held his hand out for this Melissa. She grasped his hand and he pulled her to his side.

"The pairing will be made official once the ceremony is completed," the man behind the microphone announced. "Please, bring forth concubine Samantha."

This continued on until the announcements reached Olivia. Her heartbeat suddenly pumped louder in her ears. Jesse tugged her arm, drawing her from her place on the side of the room. She took a few steps forward, trembling as ice water seemed to race through her veins and made her knees feel weak. She did not want to fall and be the one concubine in history to fall on her face.

When she and Jesse came to a stop in the center of the room, eight men stepped forward. Her eyes widened and she gripped Jesse's arm, no doubt digging her nails into his flesh again.

"Jesse," she whispered.

"You're fine," he answered.

Then, another joined the eight, bringing it to nine. Then, Victor made ten. She gasped.

"Do I have to accept him?"

"No," he whispered. "Now, be quiet."

The two men she'd had the awkward sniffing interaction with earlier were among the ten. Three other men were chatting with her two. Victor stepped forward, putting himself into her space. He sniffed her, like the others had, then stepped back and grinned. He held his hand out to her.

Her eyes widened, fear clamped on her chest, and Olivia shook her head.

Victor's smile dropped and he snarled. "You cannot defy me, concubine."

"Yes, she can," came the voice of the first familiar man. "She has the right to refuse. And she has invoked that right. Now, please, step away and allow the others to have a look."

Victor snarled and turned away from her, fading back into the crowd. She met the gaze of the dark-haired man who had spoken.

Thank you, she mouthed.

He bowed ever so slightly, acknowledging her. If he were to hold his hand out for her, she would rush to his side.

The man turned back to the crowd and confusion filled her. Did he not want her? She felt a slight pang of rejection. Then, he turned back to her, the other who sniffed her at his side. The other three who were speaking with her dark-haired man stepped forward.

One had sandy blond hair and caramel eyes. He smiled at her and stepped close. He tilted her head up with a finger under her chin and kept her gaze locked on his.

"Are you nervous?" he asked.

"Scared to death," she whispered.

He chuckled. "Don't be. You're safe here." He released her and stepped back.

Another man stepped forward and he had similar features to her dark-haired beauty. Were they brothers? His hair was longer, though, shaggy. It suited him. He tilted her head up, then side to side, examining her neck, maybe her shoulders. He smiled.

"You're stunning, my dear. Magnificent."

She smiled and felt heat creep up her cheeks. Like the others, he stepped back to his friends. One more man stepped forward. His skin was dark like chocolate. His eyes a light coffee. He smirked and nodded to her, as if saying, "'Sup?"

She grinned and shrugged a single shoulder.

He chuckled and stepped closer. Like the first two, he leaned in and smelled her. Unlike the first two, though, he lingered. "My gods, I could breathe you in all day." His voice was like a song that called to her. As he pulled away, she turned to meet his gaze. "Exquisite," he whispered. He stepped back to his friends and the five of them conversed quietly, each sending sporadic glances her way.

She cleared her throat and looked up at Jesse. She frowned at the expression of humor on his face.

"What?" she whispered.

"I told you, you're safe."

She nodded and turned back to the five men. The first one she'd met stood to the front of the five and smiled, then held his hand out to her.

"Congratulations, Miss Martin. This will be a great pairing for you," Jesse whispered.

She smiled, let go of her guard, and closed the distance to her vampire.

"My name is Jared," he offered and tucked her hand into the inside of his arm. "Allow me to introduce you to my brothers at arms."

Her brows lifted, curious. "I'm not sure I understand?" she asked.

"Miss Martin," he began.

"Olivia, please."

He nodded. "Olivia, you will not be just mine. You will be *ours.*" The other four surrounded her and suddenly five breath-stealing men encircled her.

She blinked, feeling light-headed, and her knees weakened for a different reason. "What?"

Chapter Four

WHEN OLIVIA MARTIN woke up this morning, she thought she was walking into a situation that would take her choices away, take away her reason for living. She would be a blood slave, blood bag, however anyone would refer to her. It was a choice she did not want to make, or participate in. Ever. Two hours ago, she walked through the doors to the coven and faced her destiny. She did not expect to see her destiny, however, dressed in high-end suits as if they just left a runway, and for there to be five vampires.

How the hell did this happen? How would she cater to five different vampires in one house? Five men equaled five sets of personalities, six including hers.

Did they expect to feed from her at the same time?

One every hour on the hour?

One each day of the week?

Sex.

Holy hell what about sex?

Was she expected to have sex with all five of them?

The car ride from the pairing was quiet and awkward. Should she talk? Should they talk? Should she tell them her favorite color is blue? Or she loved the sunset when the sky was pink and orange? That she had never been to Disney?

The limo was dark inside, and she sat in silence with five of the most attractive men she had ever laid eyes on. The ice in her drink clinked and damn, she realized she would need a refill quickly. She was given a vodka and tonic upon her request and currently she sipped on melted ice.

Jared, the first one she'd met tonight, had dark hair and chocolate brown eyes. He had this sex appeal about him the screamed *Bond*, like a secret agent. He was calm, cool, and laid back. She imagined sitting in his lap while he sipped from her neck, a hand in her panties.

She licked her lips and when he met her gaze, she gasped and quickly adverted her gaze. Had he just read her thoughts? She pressed her lips together and dared another glance. She caught him chuckling and the smile reached his eyes.

She grinned and looked at the man next to him, who Jared introduced to her as his brother, Jake.

Where Jared was smooth and calm, Jake appeared to be more on the reckless side. Olivia imagined him riding on a Harley down the strip, grinning, while the wind blew through his long, russet hair. His eyes were the same brown as Jared's, and Jake had a tattoo in Italian, *'famiglia'*, below it a cross and behind it, thorn vines. It was striking. She met his gaze and realized he had been watching her appraisal.

"You like what you see?" he asked her in a gruff, sexy voice.

She cleared her throat. "I like your tattoo."

He glanced down to it and nodded. "Got it before I was turned."

Jared cleared his throat and Jake looked at his brother.

She wasn't sure what was passing between them but felt it best to let it go.

"Thank you for speaking up for me," Olivia offered.

Jared leaned forward, grasped her chin, and tilted her head up. She met his gaze and once again, gasped. He leaned in so close, oh so close.

"You are welcome," he whispered. "I liked you when I first saw you before the doors even opened. I could not let such a precious jewel be tainted by the hands of one who would not appreciate her value."

Her insides melted at his words and she smiled. "Thank you."

He let her go and leaned back in his seat. "You never have to thank me. It is us, who should thank you."

"Thank me?" she asked. "Why would you ever need to thank me?"

"For offering your blood to us," came the baritone voice of one named Landon. Oh, Landon, he was absolutely sex set aflame with confidence of a man who knew how to handle a woman. His hair, black as midnight, curled slightly in its natural state, and sat just brushing his shoulders. He had what sounded like an Italian accent.

"I do not mean offense to this," she said in a soft voice. "But I do not really have a choice in the matter."

Jared raised a brow. "You always have a choice, Olivia. We all do. No one in this car will take blood from you without your approval. No one will attempt sex with you without your approval. No one will make you feel inferior. No one will do anything to you that would impact your relationship with us. That, Olivia, is a promise." Jared rested one arm over the seat of the car and motioned to the blond man in their group.

Ethan, as he called himself, offered a bottle to Jared. What was in the bottle? Booze? Blood? Do vampires bottle blood?

Olivia glanced over to the last one in the car, Aidan. His skin was like the finest of chocolates. His eyes were a light tan, almost golden color. He smirked at her, which she returned with a smile. He had this suaveness about him. She imagined him in a club, talking to three to four ladies at a time. End of the night, he would have them all go to his hotel room, together. But this was a first impression of him, not necessarily who he was.

But, then again, here they were, all six of them. One woman, five men.

A cool touch on her hand startled her, and it was Ethan. He smiled and handed her a glass, fresh with ice, vodka, and tonic. "You should not have to sip on the ice. Here you go." He took the empty glass from her.

"Thank you," she whispered, and drank almost the entire contents in one swallow. He was nice to think of her. She smiled and decided to sip on the rest.

The car turned a corner and pulled into a gated driveway. Her heart sped in rhythm and she wondered briefly if they could hear it beat. Did their hearts beat? Were they still alive? Did they have their own blood? Could they produce children?

The notion of a nursing vampire baby piercing her nipple made her cringe.

No, thank you.

Ouch.

The gate opened slowly and the car pulled through. They rode down the long drive, which felt like the Green Mile, again. As the limo pulled into the garage, Olivia's breath hitched in her chest. They were here.

Holy hell, they were here.

The car turned off and the dome light came on.

Florescent lights were never forgiving, no matter how hot someone appeared to be. You could be going to the club or coming from the club. Florescent lights ruined any kind of sex appeal.

Except for vampires.

Even under the harsh lights, the men in front of her were still stunning. She met their gazes, all eyes focused on her. She was a lamb in front of lions for the slaughter. Olivia fisted her hands by her sides and lowered her gaze. Her throat began to close on her and she coughed.

"Olivia," came a demanding voice that belonged to a man who had power. His power could dominate a room with a single command. It was Jared. "Breathe," he told her.

A hand smoothed down her back and she inhaled a sharp breath.

"You're safe. Please, trust us. No one will hurt you here."

She regarded the voice next to her. It was not the demanding one. This one was softer, elegant. It was Aidan. She stared into his golden eyes. He smiled at her, cupped her chin and tilted it up slightly.

"There you go. Just breathe. You'll be just fine. Keep breathing."

She nodded a slow nod and felt herself calming. She'd dated one man at a time in her past, but her present now had five vampires who would require her blood as sustenance to survive. How could she breathe and pretend all of this was okay?

She lowered her gaze to her lap and opened her palms. She'd dug her nails into her hands hard enough to draw blood. Fear sent a chill snaking down her spine.

Fuck me.

Blood and I'm in a car full of vampires!

Shit!

She lifted her gaze up fast and met Jared's gaze.

He frowned and tilted his head. "What's wrong?" he asked her.

"Did you forget something at your home?" Jake asked. "We can have it fetched."

"I think we need to give her a minute," Aidan answered them and sat back. "She has a bit of a wound on her hands that needs treating."

"What the hell?" Jared growled and reached for her arm.

She expected him to grab and manhandle her. Instead, he gently took her arm and turned her palm over in his hand. He shook his head, then looked into her eyes.

"We have a first aid kit in the house. Come on," he said as the door to the limo opened.

What the hell took so long?

A hand reached in and she paused.

"Miss Martin?" came the voice of the driver.

She slipped her hand into his grasp and he helped her step out. She blinked at him. "Ted?"

He grinned. "Nice to see you again, Olivia."

"I didn't know you drove for them."

"When you were picked as their concubine, I was part of the package."

"As was I," came another familiar voice.

She turned around and found Jesse. It was like having two friends join her in her new life. Well, something like friends. Jesse might be good to have around. Maybe. Maybe not. Time would tell.

She thought of her friend, Tawne. If Jesse were single, she would have to hook them up. Tawne was a friend she'd known since Kindergarten. Tawne was not aware of Olivia's future as a blood demon, or what her future entailed. When her pairing came of age, Olivia was instructed to severe ties with her family and friends. The excuse had been studying college abroad. Permanently.

Ted and Jesse moved to the trunk of the car and began to pull out Olivia's suitcases. She turned back to the car and Jared stood before her, at his full height, towering above her.

"Jesus you're tall," she whispered.

He chuckled.

"Oh shit, I said that?" she gasped and covered her mouth with her hand. Real nice.

He smirked and nodded. "It's okay." He stared at her body, focusing on her breasts for a moment, then her waist, her thighs, calves, then moved back up to her eyes. In some instances, someone undressing her with their eyes creeped her out. This was not one of those times. She became wet with need and bit her lip.

Jake stood from the car, followed by Ethan. Both men were as tall as Jared.

Jake stood to the left of Jared, Ethan to his right. They were like a trifecta of sex. Jared held his hands in front of him, Ethan had his hands on his hips, and Jake pushed his into his pockets.

Add in two more sex pistols named Landon and Aidan.

Olivia felt faint and took a step back. She felt the blood rush from her head and began to see spots.

"She's about to go down," came the concerned voice of one of the men.

Her knees gave out and just before she hit the ground, a set of thick, muscular arms grabbed her body and blackness took her sight.

***

"She's coming to."

"Bring the water over. She'll need to drink something."

"Maybe some crackers?"

"She didn't donate blood."

"Not yet," someone chuckled, followed by, "Ow! Was it necessary to slap my head?"

"Fuck yes, you moron. She fainted being in our presence. Teasing about taking her blood is not helping matters."

Olivia opened her eyes, batting her lashes a few times to clear the fog from her vision. She found Jared staring down Jake.

"Did you just joke about me donating my blood to you?"

Jared turned to her and shook his head. "No, love. That was not me." He took a seat next to her and took her hand. "Are you all right? Here, we have some water for you."

Ethan handed her a glass of water. Jared helped her sit up. She brought the cold liquid to her lips and sipped it. The relief was instant and amazing. She needed more. As she sipped, she found five sets of eyes watching her.

She felt like a fish in a bowl. She swallowed and wiped her mouth with the back of her hand. Handing the glass back to Ethan, she whispered, "Thank you."

"You're welcome," he said and squatted down. "Do you need to eat? We have plenty of food stocked."

"Maybe, but not yet. I just... I need to adjust. Please, all I ask is for your patience."

Jared stood and took his brother by his arm and left the room. Olivia watched them until they disappeared. She looked back at Ethan, then Landon, and finally Aidan. "I'm sorry."

"For what?" Landon asked and took a seat next to her. "You did nothing wrong."

"I fainted. How embarrassing."

"How about we show you to your room?" Aidan offered. He held his hand out to her.

She hesitated for a moment, then slipped her hand into his. He wore a gold ring on his index finger with a ruby in the center of it that caught her attention.

"That's a stunning ring," she offered.

Aidan turned their hands over and looked to it. "I received it when I was still human, from my father."

"Oh," she whispered. "Well, it's beautiful."

He looked at her and brushed the back of her hand with his lips. "You're beautiful."

She giggled to herself. Five men. One woman. How would she do this?

"Umm, Aidan?"

"Yes, darling?"

She grinned. "I need a few minutes to myself, if that's okay?"

"Of course," he told her. "When you're ready to come out, we'll be in the den, where we just left."

She nodded. They ascended a flight of stairs. The stairs were hardwood, like the rest of the floors. The walls were white with art work from a few artists she recognized. Vases, art pieces, and a few statues. She never knew anyone who had a statue.

Once they reached the top, they took a right turn and three doors down, Aidan opened a door. "Here you go. The room has been made up for you. It's yours now. Feel free to redecorate it as you wish, or leave it be. It's completely up to you, and it's yours."

"Oh my God," she whispered. The room was large, the size of the living room of her rental home. A king-sized, four poster bed with a sheer canopy sat in the center of the room. Each poster had a rod leading to the next. The canopy sheer twisted up each poster pole to the top, swiped once over each rod, then twisted down the next rod. It was stunning and silver. The bedcover matched the canopy sheer.

The room had a dresser, chest of drawers, a wardrobe, and a closet. Next to the dresser were her suitcases. She crossed the room and opened the closet door, then gasped. The closet was the size of a small bedroom. In the center sat a bench. Each side had shoes racks filled with shoes in her size. Heels to flats to runners; she had shoes of every style and color she could only imagine.

Dresses were on one side, tops another, pants another. It was all too much.

She turned to face a smiling Aidan, and found Jared and Jake had joined him.

"This is too much," she argued.

"Nonsense," Jared told her and stepped into the closet with her. "We wanted you comfortable and to want for nothing."

"Well, I'm pretty sure that was achieved."

He chuckled. "If there's anything you need that's not here—"

"My cat," she interrupted. "I'm sorry, I didn't mean to interrupt, but my cat, Sherlock."

"Oh, sorry, we can't do a cat," Jake chided.

Jared lifted a brow and turned to face his brother. "What?"

"Remember? I'm allergic." Jake told him.

"Seriously?" she asked. "Vampires have allergies?"

Jake grinned. "Nah, I'm kidding. Your cat is on his way."

She shook her head.

So, Jake is a jokester.

Good to know.

Jared seems a bit hardened.

Polar opposites.

"Right," she took a few steps toward the closet door. The men in there stood and did not move. She raised her brows and smiled.

"Oh," Jared moved first and chuckled. "Sorry, we'll, umm, get out of your hair. When you're ready for breakfast, come on downstairs."

"Breakfast?" she asked.

He glanced to his watch and nodded. "It's going on three am."

"Holy hell," she whispered, then yawned. Exhaustion hit when she realized the time.

"See you in a while," Jake offered.

She smiled. "Thank you."

"You're welcome," Aidan followed up and was the first to leave the room. Jake behind him.

Jared paused in the doorway with his back to her. He glanced at her over his shoulder, tossing her a deep, gruff sounding, "Welcome home." Then he left and closed the door behind him.

She walked over to the bed and pulled the covers down. She had intended to head downstairs, but the lure of that big, comfy looking bed changed her mind. She did not bother with pajamas. She was too exhausted to change. Instead, she stripped from her clothes and climbed into the cool sheets. As soon as her head hit the pillow, sleep pulled her under.

Chapter Five

OLIVIA STIRRED BETWEEN the moment of awake and asleep, the moment of vulnerability between life and death. She inhaled deep and stretched, then yawned. Expecting to find the edge of her bed, and not, she opened her eyes as fear struck her. She sat up in the bed, pulling the covers to her chest. She was naked. Why was she naked? She scanned around the room and last night's events came crashing back to her.

Concubine.

Vampires.

Pairing ceremony.

Five vampires.

Blackout boards closed off any sunshine that may peer through.

She was naked.

Five vampires.

She closed her eyes and laid back down. Olivia pulled the covers over her head and turned on her side.

She needed Tawne. She needed Sherlock. She needed... Hell, she needed someone to walk her through the motions of what was expected of her. Jesse helped last night, a lot actually. Her five new vampires appeared to have her best interest, but for how long?

Oh damn, they were so hot, beautiful, sexy as hell.

Did they sleep naked?

Jees, Liv, stop it.

She pulled the cover back down with a sigh. This life would only start if she allowed it to. She could hide in here like Belle in the Disney story, but eventually, the Beast—well. Beasts–would break down her door and drag her out, demanding her blood for their bellies.

Death by fang. Tonight, on the eleven o'clock news.

She rolled her eyes at her thoughts and slipped out of bed, her feet touching the cool hardwood. She stretched again, pushing her arms up in the air, then bent down and touched the floor. Righting herself, she opened the closet door and sighed at the sight before her.

All the clothes, shoes, handbags, everything she could ever want.

Right now, though, she needed to clean up, use the bathroom, brush her teeth and hair, and find something to eat that did not consist of a blood type.

Padding across the floor to the bathroom, she flipped on the light and sighed in relief that it was a single use bathroom, not a Jack & Jill. She could not imagine walking in on a vampire, or one of them walking in on her.

She imagined the fright if one of them found her on the pot. The thought actually made her giggle. Olivia shook her head and turned the corner in the bathroom, to what could only be described as a goddess's bathroom.

She also had a vanity, complete with a chair, three-way mirror lit with Hollywood style bulbs, jewelry boxes that held necklaces, rings, and bracelets. Different eye shadows, lipsticks, and blushes were also laid out. The setup took up an entire wall of her bathroom.

A shower, large enough to not need doors, had five showerheads. *Five!* One on top that was long like a rectangle, and four along the wall. It was large enough to hold seven to eight people, easily. Olivia imagined her standing in the middle of the five men in the house as water sluiced down from above.

Her knees weakened, and she pressed a hand to the wall. She closed her eyes and inhaled deep, then let it go. She turned on the shower and the rectangular showerhead rained down water. It reminded her of the fountain in sky at the palace of Versailles in France. Just a much smaller scale. She found a few towels and set them on what appeared to be a towel warmer.

She stepped under the showerhead. The water was perfect. She closed her eyes and allowed the memories of yesterday to wash down the drain. Today would be a new day. She would put her best foot forward every day to make this work. She was a female in a pool full of testosterone.

***

Olivia opened the door to her room and peeked out, not sure if someone would be guarding her door or not. She opted for halter dress that was the color of butter with a matching shrug. She found comfortable wedge sandals and wore her hair down. She considered pulling it up but figured that may appear to be an invitation to bite her.

But, then again, she was stereotyping.

Gripping the handrail, she descended the stairs. The house was quiet. Too quiet. The silence was broken only by the ticking of a grandfather clock at the bottom of the stairs. She glanced at the hands: eight am. The clock was old, very old. The wood had been resealed maybe a few years ago, but whoever took care of this clock had a lot of love for it.

Then, the smell of bacon called to her. She inhaled and her belly growled. She turned and followed the mouthwatering aroma through the white-walled halls of the house, past the portraits and paintings, and it led her to the kitchen. The kitchen was gourmet, huge, with a large island in the middle with barstools. There was a breakfast nook with six chairs.

The familiar pop and sizzle of bacon frying was found, and with it, one of her vampires. From the backside she knew it was Jake. And by backside, he was impressive. He wore a fitted white tank with boxer shorts. And nothing else. She salivated at the sight of him. Still hungry for food, but she wanted something more.

Instead, she made no sound to alert him she was there and turned to leave. She was not invited to partake and did not want to assume. Although, now that she knew where the kitchen was, she would be back here very soon.

"Don't leave," Jake called to her.

She turned to face him, but his back was still to her. "How did you know I was here?"

He glanced over his shoulder at her and smiled. "I could feel you."

She blinked. "Come again? Feel me?"

"Yeah," he answered her. "How do you like your eggs?"

"Sunny side down, medium. Lightly salted," she told him. Olivia pulled out a stool and took a seat.

Jake cracked two eggs open and fried them in the bacon grease. He salted them then turned to face her. He lifted his brows. "The dress, wow." He shook his head with a smile. "Talk about good morning."

She felta blush creep to her cheeks and looked down at the counter. "Thank you."

"Did you sleep okay?" He turned back to the eggs and finished up, then plated the eggs for her, with a healthy serving of perfectly crisped bacon.

"I don't think I moved, actually," she said and picked up her fork. "Thank you for breakfast."

"You're welcome." He crossed his arms over his chest and watched her.

She felt exposed and stopped chewing. She swallowed the food and prayed she would not choke. Clearing her throat, she asked, "Are you going to eat?"

He shook his head no. "We do not eat food."

Olivia raised her brows, glanced down at her food, then at him. "You did this for me?"

He nodded. "Yes, of course." He said it as if she should have known. As if it were his duty to please her, serve her.

"I feel awkward eating in front of you," she whispered.

"I can turn around?" And he did.

She grinned. "No, don't do that." Jake turned back to face her with a smile of his own. His features were striking, like a movie star meets president of a motorcycle club. Yes, Jake was pure sex. "Talk to me while I eat?"

He nodded. "Sure. What would you like to talk about?"

She took in her plate of food thought of cooking. "How did you learn to cook?"

"When I was still a human, I did not get much of a chance to work in the kitchen. We were at war."

"Which war?" She thought maybe desert storm, or something more recent.

"World War II."

Her eyes widened. "No! Seriously?"

He nodded. "Yes. Jared and I both were in the war. We're originally from Tennessee. We enlisted to fight. Jared was captured as a prisoner of war. He was..." Jake trailed off, smiled, and lowered his gaze to the floor. "He'll tell you his story when he's ready. Anyway, I was shot and laid on my deathbed, waiting to die. I remember opening my eyes and seeing my brother standing above me. I thought I'd died and he was meeting me to bring me to the pearly gates. Jared bent down and whispered he was going to save my life. He bit his arm and blood trickled from it. He pressed his wrist to my mouth. I was too weak to fight him off. Hours later, I was changed. He saved me and gave me this new life."

Listening to his story, Olivia had not moved or blinked. "Wow," she whispered. "So, your age freezes, then, to the moment you're changed?"

He nodded.

This information about Jared and Jake provided a new aspect about the siblings. Jared was not ready to let Jake go. Jake had been with his brother ever since. That's either love between brothers, or punishment. Jared loved his brother enough to want to offer him this life or hated him to the point of retribution and forced this upon him. From what she could see, it was the former.

Silence passed between them for a moment as she finished her breakfast. Her belly felt full and she finished her orange juice. She stood to take her plate to the sink when Jake took it from her.

"No, allow me. Please, you're our guest."

She sat back onto her stool and contemplated what he meant by her being their guest. At what point would this change? When would she feel like she belonged versus being a blood demon forced against her will to be here?

At least they were kind toward her. It could have been much worse. She could have ended up with Victor.

Jake walked around the island and took the stool seat next to her. He rested his hands on the counter, then met her gaze. "Do you enjoy cooking?"

She smiled, then giggled. The giggle then became a laugh. She wiped at her eyes and snorted.

"What did I say?" he asked with a chuckle.

"This entire thing," she said and motioned between them. "I have moved into a house with five men, I have no idea what to do or say, and you're asking me if I enjoy cooking. I'm sorry, but it made me laugh because, honestly, I don't know if I should laugh or cry at this situation."

He reached for her hands and squeezed them in his. His touch was cool, his hands soft. She wasn't sure what to expect from a vampire's touch, but she was surprised it relaxed her.

"You can do whatever it is you feel you need to do. We are in this with you. We have been together for a while now as brothers. We typically share everything and decided a long time ago, when we found our concubine, we would also share her. So, please, not knowing what to say or do, where to go, or expectations, trust me, we're there with you."

She sighed and offered a smile. "I appreciate that, Jake." She pulled one of her hands away from his hold and wiped at her eyes. "I love baking. I wanted to become a pastry chef. I love decorating desserts and creating something exquisite out of nothing."

He nodded. "As beautiful as you are, I would love to see what beauty would come from you."

Then something Jake said to her earlier struck her curious. She wanted to know more. "Jake?"

He smirked. "I like hearing you say my name."

She blushed and fidgeted with her fingers. "Will you tell me what you meant by 'feeling me'?"

"Sure," he started and picked up the orange juice, then refilled the glass. "Every vampire has a type of ability. Most of us are very fast in speed. It is seldom one is not."

She nodded. "Can you read minds?"

He chuckled and shook his head. "No, we do not read minds. We do, however, pick up on the moods around us. For instance, if you were upset, we could feel the current shift in the mood around you. Imagine the calm before the storm. The air around you would feel normal. Then, as your anger rose, so would the aura around you. It could be fierce, like a virtual slap."

"Wow, okay." She wanted to ask about being turned on, finding one of them sexy, like Jake, who stood almost naked before her in a fitted tank and his underwear. She felt her cheeks blush and when she met his gaze, he grinned. "What about being turned on?"

"This is my favorite to explore."

"Oh?" she asked and leaned on the island toward him.

He nodded and leaned closer to her. "I could feel you, as if your body called out for mine." The pads of his fingertips played across her cheek, like she were a violin and he caressed her strings. "I could feel you across the house and know exactly where to find you."

She swallowed hard and her lips parted. She wanted to kiss him, but she also wanted to back away and put space between them. Itching for more information, she continued on. "How can you tell when this happens? Is it..." she did not want to compare herself to a dog but went with it. "My smell?"

He grinned. "Yes, precisely."

She nodded. "So, if I were in my room, and I wanted you, and you were, let's say, outside or maybe at the store. You could feel me calling for you?"

He leaned in closer. She could see specs of gold in the brown of his eyes. "I could feel you across the globe and would come to you as fast as my speed would carry me."

"Oh," she whispered.

His fingertips traced a soft line from her cheek to her neck. She closed her eyes and tilted her head for him. He cupped one side of her cheek in his palm and lightly pressed his forehead to hers. "I would love to kiss you," he whispered.

"Would that make it weird for the others, if you kiss me?"

"Not in the least. Each of us want you, Olivia. Not just for your blood."

As if the word blood woke her, she opened her eyes and pulled away from him. She took a deep breath and kept her eyes downcast. "I don't... I... I don't know what to do."

He touched her chin and lifted her head up. She met his gaze and Jake smiled. "In time, it will come naturally to you. I promise you this, Olivia Martin. We are your stable and each of us, your personal stallion."

This statement sent a shiver of excitement, longing, and a desperate need for sex throughout her body. Jake picked up on it and leaned in closer to her once more.

"I'm scared," she whispered.

"Let yourself go and we'll be there to catch you every single time."

A ragged breath pushed through her lips and she closed her eyes. "Kiss me," she told him.

Jake tilted her chin up just enough to anticipate his lips touching hers. "Open your eyes," he whispered.

A tear slipped down her cheek. Her heart sped and she felt her lip tremble.

"Olivia, please, open your eyes."

Her resolve melted away and she opened her eyes. She met his gaze and felt a mixture of relief and gratefulness rush through her.

Jake cupped her face, but he was not close enough to kiss her.

"I want you to want this, not feel obligated. I do not want you scared. I want your panties melting, your body trembling, your entire being needing every one of us like the touch of us would save you from the burning of the sun. I will never take from you what is not honestly and freely given."

And with that, he released her and took a step back. He motioned toward the entrance. "You are welcome to move about the house, anywhere you like. I'm usually in the billiards area kicking everyone's ass. So, you've been warned. I'm good."

She nodded and wanted to go to him, hug him for being a gentleman. "Then I'll take your word on it. I suck at pool. Maybe you can teach me sometime?"

He nodded. "I'd love to put my arms around you and show you how to hold a stick the right way." He winked and she laughed out loud.

"Yeah, I see what you did there."

Jake smiled once more, then turned to leave.

"Jake?" she called after him.

He stepped back into the kitchen. "Yes?"

"Come here." The nerves that messed with her earlier disappeared. Was she still scared? Hell, yes. Did she want to kiss Jake? Absolutely.

He strode up to her and towered over her small size. "Yes, ma'am?"

His size did not intimidate her. Olivia reached for him and slipped her arms around his neck. She pulled him down to her and brushed her lips across his mouth.

Jake cupped her cheeks in both his large hands. His tongue traced the seam of her lips and she opened her mouth for him. His tongue teased hers. He groaned and moved his hands to her waist and pulled her close, her body flush against his.

Olivia gasped and pulled back from the kiss but did not pull away from him. "Thank you," she told him.

He grinned. "For what?"

"For being honest, listening to me, and your patience."

"You're welcome." Jake pressed his lips to hers once, then rested his forehead on hers. "I need to stop or I fear I may feed from you."

Her body went from hot to cold in a second. Her stance stiffened, and she took a step back.

Jake released her and he kept his gaze to the floor. He turned away from her and quickly strode out of the kitchen.

She sat down on the barstool and sighed. What would she do with Jake now that they had kissed?

What about the others?

Well?

Only way to find out is to go meet them.

She was not sure who she may run into next when she left the kitchen. She walked down the hall and it opened into the main room of their house. Statues, portraits, paintings...and in the middle of the grand room stood was a dual staircase of wrought iron framing, a water fountain. Marble in white coloring with gray accents, it was wide enough to step into, with three tiers. It stood close to seven feet in height. Water ran over the edges of each tier to collect in the large basin at the bottom. It was magnificent with a wrought iron chandelier above it. The make matched the staircase with twenty-four candle bulbs, twelve on the outer circle, and twelve on the inner.

"Care for a walk?"

She turned to find Ethan approaching. She nodded. "Yes, please."

Chapter Six

WHEN THE BIG bad wolf approaches, Red Riding Hood should feel frightened. However, the wolf, or in this case sexy-as-sin vampire that approached Olivia caused her to tremble in the most delectable way. She did not feel frightened when he stood before her.

A light gray button down dress shirt strained over his thick pecs, tapered at his waist before leading to pressed midnight-black trousers and polished

Testoni Italian leather dress shoes. The shirt sleeves were halfway rolled to the elbows, a gold Armani watch graced his wrist. She felt like the devil himself stepped into the room, home to claim his prize for the evening. The thought sent a delicious shiver snaking up her spine and a heat to build in her core.

She motioned to the fountain. "I have never been in a home with a fountain on the inside. It is truly beautiful."

"Ahh, yes, *Marie*," Ethan called her. "We had her installed a few years ago. She brings a sound to the silence that most days envelops our home."

Olivia nodded and lowered her gaze. "You named her Marie?"

He nodded. "Have you toured much of the home?" he asked.

She shook her head. "I found the kitchen and Jake cooked for me."

"Oh good. I was hoping you had food. How was your meal?"

"It was great."

He offered his arm to her and she grasped it. She felt the muscle in his bicep and it flexed a few times. She wondered what he would look like with no shirt. Hell, *naked.* The idea sent a rush of heat to her core. The fit of his clothes did not leave much to the imagination, in the best way possible.

He cleared his throat and she blushed.

Right, emotions.

"So, Jake likes to cook. What do you do for fun?"

"Well," He turned toward a room for entertainment. "I wouldn't call it fun, but I'm a lawyer. Our family lawyer."

"Oh," she said and looked up at him. "Just for your brothers here?"

"Mostly, and I do some work with the coven when needed. I don't think any of that will interest you, though, contracts and such."

She wrinkled her nose and shook her head. "No, sorry. No offense intended."

He smiled. "None taken. Tell me about you?" Ethan said. They walked into the room and inside was the billiard table Jake spoke of. Were they going to play pool? There was a bar with many bottles of liquor. She grew curious.

"Ethan?"

He turned to her and raised his brows.

"Do vampires drink liquor?"

"Sometimes. It tastes like it did as a human, but it has no effects on us."

"Wow, well, that's no fun."

He chuckled. "Well, I should say that's partly true. If you were inebriated, and we drank from you, the alcohol in your blood would cause us to become drunk with you. But, it would take a large quantity of blood to do so."

Blood?

A lot of her blood?

She let go of his arm and took a step back, nausea boiling up from her belly, a lump lodging in her throat. She felt sick.

"Olivia," Ethan started. "I'm not going to suggest you drink and we take your blood. I would never do such a thing. That is barbaric. Also, when you're ready to feed us, we'll take it slow, easy, baby steps."

She met his gaze and shook her head. "I hate needles."

He raised a brow. "Well, that was random but understandable. I hate needles, too. I could never stand being pierced, poked, or any of the sort. Hated it." He held his hand open for her. "Please, join me. I'd like to show you something."

She hesitated for a moment, then decided to slip her hand into his. Like Jake's, Ethan's hand was soft. He brought her hand up and brushed his lips across the back of it. "Please, do not fear what you do not know," he whispered. "You're safe here."

She nodded and lowered her gaze. "I... I have trust issues."

He touched under her chin and tilted her head up. She met his gaze, his eyes a piercing blue. "I would think something off about you if you didn't."

She didn't expect that, and it caught her off guard. She laughed. "Well, it didn't help growing up an only child, my mother being an only child, not knowing who my father was except he's an incubus, and no cousins. When my mother died, I became an orphan in this world. I have no one."

"Not true," he whispered. "You have all five of us."

Her heart melted a little bit. Her hard resolve began to weaken, and soon the fortress that surrounded her would come crumbling down. She hoped her five men would be there to catch her when she fell.

Ethan reached for the door in the room and turned the knob. What would be on the other side?

A dungeon full of whips and chains?

A movie theater?

A dark room?

He pulled the door open and stepped inside. She remained outside until the lights flickered on. She gasped and her mouth opened wide.

It was a private study filled with books, a desk, and a computer.

An actual computer.

She did not have any way of reaching out through email, social media, anything, until now.

"Oh, Ethan, is this yours or does everyone have access?" She stepped further in and admired the books on the dark wooden shelves. She could not tell what order they were in. Not alphabetical by title or by author. Maybe in order of when they were acquired?

"Everyone has access. I do most of my work in here. Behind the desk are my law books. Other than that, we've all collected things here and there, and store the artifacts here."

She tugged on a spine that read, '*And Then There Were None,*' by *Agatha Christie.* She opened it and gasped.

"A signed copy?" She turned to face Ethan and he grinned.

"Yes, I was able to secure a signed copy. I did not meet her, but this copy she had signed. I felt it a piece of history and wanted it."

"Understandable," she whispered and slipped it back on the shelf. "Do I have free reign to this room as well?" she dared ask, glancing over her shoulder at the vampire in the room.

He took a few steps closer to her and stood just next to her. "Yes, of course. Everything we have is now yours."

"I can use the computer as well?"

He nodded. "Of course."

She felt a weight lift off her shoulders. Maybe she would not be alone after all. "Am I able to invite friends over to visit?"

"Only a few trusted associates know where our home is. Unfortunately, we do not cater to many people. However, I'll bring the topic up to the brothers."

"Is it like a majority vote kind of thing?"

He shook his head. "No, not quite. If we decide it is safe for you to see your friends, we'll arrange a location for you to meet. It would not be here. However, we have associates we do trust who have companions. I'm happy to arrange a meeting if you may have questions you'd like to ask a fellow concubine?"

She considered this for a moment. Turning back to the books, she walked along the length of the wall, lightly touching the books on the shelves. Some old, some newer, so many ready to be read. She paused, then turned to face him. He had not followed her. She raised her brow and as if a cue had been given, he crossed the room and stood at her side.

Hmm, interesting.

"I would like to meet with your friends and their...err...person."

He nodded. "Then I'll arrange it." Ethan took another step closer to her and raised a hand to touch her cheek, but hesitated. "May I?"

She nodded. "Yes."

He brushed a few strands of hair behind her ear, then trailed his finger gently over her ear, to her throat, and jaw line.

She closed her eyes and allowed herself to enjoy this intimacy between them. "Jake told me about the emotions you're able to pick up on."

"Did he?" he asked, his heated breath caressing her neck.

She gasped, not realizing Ethan had leaned in.

His breath fanned over her ear and he cupped the other side of her face. "I would love to kiss you, seduce you, touch the most intimate parts of your body until you're begging for me to enter you."

She swallowed and tightened her fingers, digging her fingers into his forearms. She had not realized she grabbed him until the pressure shot through her hands. A soft mewling sounded between them. When her lips parted, she realized it was her who made the sound.

"May I kiss you, Olivia?" he asked. "I would love to taste your lips."

"Oh my," she whispered. She turned her face toward his and before she could say yes, his lips were on hers. His kiss alone made her wet, her panties drenched with need. She pressed her thighs together in hopes to keep herself from catching fire. Heat coursed through her body and Ethan pressed her back to the bookcase.

He growled against her lips and moved his lips to her jaw line, then nibbled on her ear.

She panted, pressing her body against his. She wanted him, needed him, more than she realized. She wanted him to consume her.

"Ethan," she whispered. "Please, we need to stop."

Ethan did not push her. He stopped as she asked and rested his forehead on her shoulder. As a vampire, he did not need air to breathe, or so she thought, but that did not stop Ethan from panting.

"I'm sorry," he whispered.

"No, don't be. I'm not... I'm afraid to... I don't think..." She could not finish her thought.

"It's okay," he said and pulled away from her. "Once you're here for a while, and know there is nothing to fear, letting go will be complete liberation, freeing, euphoric."

She nodded and lowered her gaze. "I'm sorry," she said again. "I'm not quite ready for this, but in time, I'm sure I will be." Her heart told her this was a lie. Her mind and body wanted her to move forward, full throttle.

She sucked in a deep breath then let it go in a rush. "Ethan, tell me about yourself. Let me get to know you, outside of being a lawyer."

He nodded, turned away from her, and crossed the room to his desk. He turned and sat on the edge of it. Crossing his arms over his chest, he raised his brows. "Where to begin?"

"How about how you met Jared, Jake, and the others?"

He remained silent for a stretch. Olivia walked over to where he sat and took a seat in one of the visitor chairs. She crossed her legs and stared up at the man before her.

He seemed focused and Olivia wondered what memories he may share with her. What would she find out about this man?

"Well, during World War II, we met on the field. We were under a storm of fire. We were on the losing side. One of the trucks used as a barricade had exploded. Men were running left and right to escape the fire of the vehicle and the gunshots. Jared was a few feet from me and he tripped, falling in front of me. The enemy ran up and pointed his rifle at Jared's head. He never saw me and did not see the bullet coming for his head. The enemy soldier fell backward, a hole in the back of his head. Jared turned over and saw me hunched over him. He thanked me and stuck by my side the rest of the time there. We had each other's backs from that point forward.

"Years later, I retired from the service, but we kept in touch. I had not realized it at the time, but after I retired, post-traumatic stress disorder caught up to me. I was in a bad place for a long time. Lots of booze, sex, women... I'm surprised I didn't kill myself with alcohol poisoning."

Olivia reached for his hand and held it in hers.

He met her gaze and continued. "Not too long after that, I was at a bachelor party. My friend was getting married. I had too much to drink and caused a fight. Someone pulled a gun and aimed it my way. I was immediately back in the war, enemies surrounding me. You could say I lost my mind, temporarily.

"Jared showed at up at the hospital. The bullet was centimeters from my heart. I was in a coma. I was dying. I don't think I would have made it through the night. Jared allowed me to die, so he could give me eternal life."

Olivia did not blink, breathe or move the entire duration of his story. She stood when he finished his story and wrapped her arms around his neck and hugged him.

"I'm so sorry," she whispered.

He hugged her back and buried his face in her shoulder. "There's nothing to be sorry about," he whispered.

She held onto him for a long moment. No fear of him biting her, seducing her, wanting to get into her panties. Just a man, holding onto a woman. A vulnerable man who opened his heart, his mind, his very being to someone he barely knew. Ethan was the bravest person she had ever met.

She pulled back just enough to look into his eyes. "Thank you for sharing this with me. I feel like I know you much better."

He smirked. "You know my background. I could be a serial killer."

She laughed. "Only if it contains milk and you spoil it for everyone else."

He blinked, then realized what she meant, and chuckled. "Gotcha. I'll make sure everyone knows I'm a cereal killer then, and the Rice Krispies will be done for."

She laughed softly. "Good to know." This time, Olivia leaned in and swept her lips across Ethan's. He quickly took over. He was soft and gentle. Not demanding and seduction driven.

The more she learned about the men in this house, the more she wanted them with her, on her, and in her. She pondered all five of them feeding on her, licking and sucking on her body. She shivered.

"Pray tell what are you thinking? Because you shivered, and your aura shifted quite dramatically. It pulled to me, and damned if it didn't feel like a wall of pheromones."

"Oh shit," she whispered. "I keep forgetting about that." She bit her lip and Ethan chuckled.

"I would love to hear what's on your mind right now."

She blushed, and Ethan grinned once more. "I was picturing in my head all five of you feeding on me at once." She hid her face and giggled. Like a schoolgirl, giggled.

Ethan tilted her head up once more and stared into her eyes. "When this happens, and trust me, Olivia, it will happen, you will want each of us on you, and you will ask for us. I would not be surprised if you were begging."

She guffawed, her mouth wide open. She shook her head and pulled away from him. "You're unbelievable," she teased with a laugh.

He shrugged. "I would say, let's make a bet, but I don't gamble."

"I do, though," came another male's voice.

Olivia and Ethan turned to find Landon entering the study.

"I would love to take that bet and prove you wrong, Olivia," Landon teased.

She grinned and leaned against the desk. Behind her, Ethan placed his hands on her waist. Landon closed the distance to her and met her gaze. He shifted his sight past her, most likely looking at Ethan. He then redirected his gaze to her, and grinned.

Olivia glanced at Ethan, then at Landon. She had two men surrounding her and felt her body temperature rise. "What just happened? What just passed between you two?"

"Nothing," Landon said with a slight accent. "Well, nothing you don't want to happen." He stepped closer and brushed his fingertips across her cheeks, then tilted her head up with a finger under her chin.

His eyes were a dark brown with hazel specs. His hair curled slightly around his face, touching his shoulders. Landon was the epitome of a sex god.

She was sandwiched between Landon and Ethan. A part of her wanted this, but her heart screamed at her to move before it became too much.

She felt Ethan brush his lips across her shoulder. A sensation flitted through her body and her clit throbbed. Landon smirked and leaned in. He tilted her head and pressed his lips to her cheek.

She closed her eyes and her pussy tingled, needing both of them inside her, their fangs in her skin. Her lips parted and she sighed. Olivia pressed her palms to Landon's chest, then pushed against him. She then sidestepped away from the men.

"I'm going to combust soon if I don't get air," she said as she fanned her face. She glanced between the two men. Both were polar opposites in features but were twins with the Cheshire grins they wore.

"While you cool down," Landon offered, "why not take a walk with me? I'll show you my studio."

She grinned. "I would love that." She turned to Ethan. "Thank you for sharing your story."

He bowed his head with a smile. "You're welcome, and same to you."

She slipped her hand into the crook of Landon's arm. The two left the confines of the study and headed toward his studio.

What would she be in for now? Did he paint canvas or did he paint nudes? She would not mind being the centerpiece for his art if it meant his hands on her. She grinned at the possibilities.

Chapter Seven

WHEN ONE WALKS the art exhibits, one typically stops to view and admire the artwork. Olivia admired each painting they passed, curious if Landon painted them, or if they were commissioned art pieces, or maybe bought from dealers.

Olivia's typical art gallery experience consisted of art supply stores and the occasional cruise. She was green when it came to knowing art, but could recognize a familiar piece by the artist work, like

Michael Cheval, Pinot, or Peter Max. The most obvious telltale she could decipher was van Gogh. The art was peculiar, and she loved his work. His story was also tragic, suicide before his work was recognized for its beauty.

She glanced over to Landon and he smiled, catching her gaze.

"I'm looking forward to sharing a part of my life with you, Olivia," he told her, his accent rounding on the r's.

She nodded. "I'm looking forward to learning something new. I'm familiar with some art, but honestly, this is new territory for me."

"I believe all of this is new for you, no?" he asked and cupped her hand on his arm. "I believe I speak for all of us that we are eager to teach you everything you need to know."

She blushed and grinned. They strolled in rhythm, one no faster than the other. Like a heartbeat in unison. She found herself inching closer to him, wanting to have him close to her without smothering him.

This is odd.

I am not the PDA person, yet, I want him to hold me.

I want them all to touch me.

What has changed?

Hell, what is wrong with me?

Landon chuckled.

She lifted her gaze up at him and frowned. "What's so funny?"

Shit, can he read thoughts?

"Something shifted in your thoughts. Imagine a pot of water hot from boiling, then suddenly it exhales a cold breath."

"I didn't think water could exhale?"

He grinned and winked at her. "Figure of speech. What I mean is, you were hot, then suddenly you felt cold."

"Oh, I didn't mean—"

He shook his head and cut her off. Landon turned Olivia to face him in the hallway. "I did not mean cold in the sense of distant. Something changed in your mindset and that is what I picked up on. Something humored you, that is all."

She gave him a crooked grin and shrugged one shoulder. "I find myself wanting to be held, wanting to be touched. But Landon," She met his gaze. "I'm not the PDA type."

"PDA?" he asked.

"Public display of affection."

"Ahh," he said and stepped closer. He slipped his hands over her waist and around her lower back. "So, what you're saying is no one has affected you as much as we have? No one has drawn out your inner sexual demon?"

She raised a brow and rested her palms on his chest. She smirked. "I may be a demon but I'm not a sex demon. If I were, I believe every one of you would be a heap of trouble."

He chuckled. "Maybe so, but just because you're a blood demon does not mean you cannot be a sex demon as well." He leaned in closer, his nose grazing hers. "You will never know until you try."

Her breath rasped as she exhaled, her mouth slightly agape. If she were to lift her head just enough, her lips would capture his. And she wanted him to kiss her.

Instead, he pressed his lips to her forehead. She'd heard once that if a man kissed you on the forehead, there was something more in that relationship. He did not want to be just friends. He wanted something more. It was a direct reflection of his feelings for you. Men did not generally do this with female friends, and if he does this with you, you mean more to him than everyone else. The endearment warmed her heart.

Olivia leaned into his shoulder as they continued their walk. They eventually turned a corner and toward the end of the corridor was an open room of color among the white walls of the home.

"Is that it down there?" she asked.

He nodded. "Yes, ahead is my studio."

"What do you prefer to paint?" She once again imagined naked women laid across a couch with a shawl so sheer it did nothing to hide from the imagination. A part of her felt almost jealous.

"You shall see when we enter. I prefer subjects I can fully immerse myself in."

She wondered if that was a double entendre. Rather than asking, she decided to accept that was exactly what he meant. Olivia knew then she would love to be the subject of one of his paintings. She felt heat creep up her neck to her ears and cheeks.

"What are you thinking, my Olivia," Landon asked.

She blushed and shifted her gaze up at him. "I like that."

"What is that?" he asked and interlaced his hand with hers.

"'My Olivia'," she quoted.

"Ahh, well then, I shall refer to you as mine, if that is okay?"

She lightly shrugged in a playful manner. "I don't see where it would hurt?" She let go of his hand and took a few steps away. The fear that once claimed her was no more than a faint ember of a fire put out by the fiercest of storms. She smoked from the sizzle, she felt the heat, but the fear had been extinguished.

As they stepped into the studio, portraits hung on the wall, a few on easels, small-sized to full-sized statues were stood in each corner and throughout the room. She noted one piece had a few obscure pieces that appeared to be boxes painted over circles. She tilted her head, then moved to the next piece. It was a woman who held a pumpkin with a small pup at her feet. The sun held in the sky and Landon managed to capture light in his art.

"I like this one. It is sweet."

"Then it is yours," he whispered behind her.

"Thank you," she said and turned to face him. "I'd like to leave it down here so I may look up on it when I come see you?"

"Of course," he told her and took her hand, then pressed his lips upon it. He turned it over and brushed his lips over her palm, then the inside of her wrist.

Their gazes met when he looked up at her. The darkness of his eyes was surrounded by a faint gold, as if encircled by it. She glanced across the room, and gasped. "Oh, Landon," she said and let go of his hand. She crossed the room and gazed upon a portrait of the beach with a woman and child. The woman held the babe in her arms, the child sleeping on his mother's shoulder. The mother held her son close, her eyes closed. Olivia could almost feel the humidity of the beach and the salt from the sea. "This is absolutely beautiful."

Landon placed his hands on her waist and she felt him step up behind her. "I recalled a memory of my mother as she walked on the beach in Italy. She carried my brother like this. It was so long ago, it worried me I would forget who they were."

She turned in his arms and wiped a tear from her eyes. "Art has never affected me, not like this. I always thought art was something nice. But this," She turned back to the portrait. "This makes me weak. It makes me want to sink to my knees and cry for your mother."

"Why?" he asked and turned her back to face him. "What draws you in so?"

She shook her head. "I never had a close relationship with my mother. Her dying words to me were, 'forgive me.' Not knowing my father, I have nothing to compare this love to." She glanced back to the portrait and felt her heart break. "It hurts," she whispered.

Landon turned her once more to face him. He cupped her face in his palm and offered an endearing smile. "*Mio amore,* art should have this kind of impact on a person. You never know how something will affect you until you find the one that wins you over. I am grateful to have had that moment for you."

She leaned into his embrace, resting her head on his chest. She loved his endearment of 'my love', in Italian. He hugged her to his body and she slipped her arms around his waist.

Landon felt comfortable, familiar, and passionate. Where Jake loved to experiment with food, and Ethan his legal work, Landon loved experimenting with emotions of art. She closed her eyes and felt safe.

Then she furrowed her brows. She was always curious about a heartbeat in vampires but heard nothing. She pulled away just enough to look into his eyes.

"Landon, I have a weird question to ask."

"Hmm, maybe I'll have a weird answer," he teased.

She smirked. "No heartbeat?"

Landon focused on her for a moment, then shook his head. "Oh, *si*, no. Vampires do not have hearts." His r's rolled and it was sexy as hell.

"No hearts? There is nothing there?"

"Oh no, love, no thump-thump." He patted on his chest.

Olivia grinned. Some were fighters, but not Landon. What she picked up from him was all lover. She imagined he took his time with his conquest. He would woo her, seduce her, touch and taste every inch of her body before he considered penetration of fangs or cock.

Her knees weakened, and a soft groan bubbled up from her throat.

He raised his brows. "Are you alright, *mio amore*?"

She blushed and her eyes widened. Had she just moaned in front of him? She quickly turned away and closed her eyes.

Holy hell, how do I recover from this?

She covered her face with her hands and erupted in a giggle fit.

Hands rested upon her shoulders and Landon feathered his mouth over the side of her neck. "You are most adorable, *mio amore*."

She shook her head. "I was lost in my own thoughts and apparently became carried away."

Landon turned her to face him. He brushed a few loose strands from her face then leaned in and pecked her cheek. *"Dimmi il mio amore cosa desideri?"* he whispered.

She did not need a translator to understand what Landon had asked. She inhaled a long breath and held it for a moment, then slowly exhaled. "What do I desire?"

He nodded. *"Sì."*

She lowered her gaze.

He clicked his tongue and shook his head no. He pointed to his eyes and winked.

She smirked.

"Okay, I want all of this. I want all of you. How can one person be drawn toward more than one person? It makes no sense to me. How can this be possible? How can I love more than one person? How can I want more than one person?"

He took a few small steps toward her. Without realizing it, Landon had moved them toward his studio wall. The chill of the wall was a welcome relief to the heat rising in her body. "You were meant to love and be adored by all of us." He ran his fingertips down the length of her arms, to her hands, then back up along her sides. "I wish to kiss and taste every bit of your body." He leaned in and peppered kisses along her jaw line, then her earlobe. "I speak for all of us, we all wish to taste you."

Her breathing rasped, her chest rose and fell in a rapid pulse. She pushed her fingers through the soft curls of his hair, pulling him closer to her. Her head rested back against the wall and she exposed her neck to him. She wanted him to bite her, to taste her, to claim her. No, she wanted *all* of them to claim her.

"Landon," she breathed. "We need to stop. I need you to stop. I don't know if I can."

He chuckled softly against her neck, pressed his mouth over the spot where her vein pulsed in her neck, then pulled away. "I would not push you further than this without my brothers here. How unfair would it be to taste you first?"

She wrapped her arms around her waist. She felt exposed, naked. She also wanted him back, them naked, with her legs wrapped around his waist. She wanted to feel him thrusting inside her as he bit her neck.

Olivia walked past him with a long, heavy sigh. "I think I need to go for a swim in the pool." She turned back to Landon. "There is a pool?"

"*Si*," he said. "I'll walk you there."

She shook her head no. "I'll find my way. I need a moment alone to gather my thoughts. So much has happened, and changed, in the last few days. I need a moment to process it all."

He nodded and took a few steps toward her. "Understood. It is indoor, southeast part of the mansion. Or facing the back of the house, on your right."

She nodded. "Thank you." Olivia turned away from her Italian stallion. She giggled to herself as she thought of the Italian actor in the boxer movies.

My stable of men.

My oh my, I have my hands full.

Olivia found her way back to her room. She opened the drawers in her dresser and found a few different swimsuits. She opted for a black two-piece. She changed into the suit, put on black sandals, and found a sheer cover-up.

Following the directions Landon provided, she tugged the cover-up around her body. She found it almost pointless. The garment was see-through. Who was she kidding? She walked toward the east part of the home and followed the corridors to the indoor pool.

The Olympic-sized pool was empty and ready for her arrival. She kicked off her shoes, removed her cover-up, then walked to the edge. She imagined briefly she swam for the US swim team, and dove in. She swam for a moment, then turned onto her back and floated. She closed her eyes and sighed in relaxation. Silence enveloped her and it was almost deafening.

She missed her cat and hoped, soon, Sherlock would be here. He would be the familiar part of herself she left behind as a concubine.

Olivia recalled the pairing ceremony. Two of the men here smelled her and knew they wanted her. She almost met Victor. The evil in his glare haunted her, even now. But he was not here, only her stable of men. She imagined the five of them in the pool with her. Her clit tingled and she wanted to touch herself, to release the orgasm that begged to be set free.

She moved to bring her hand down her body, over her breast to her belly, when she heard someone clear their throat.

Olivia gasped and found Aidan and Jared staring down at her. Aidan smirked whereas Jared simply stared. She swam toward the ladder and grabbed hold of it to climb out.

"No, please, don't stop on account of us," Aidan told her.

She blushed and wanted to hide under the water.

Why can't I be a mermaid and swim away?

"Leave her be," Jared told him and walked toward the ladder. He squatted down and touched her hand. "I hear you've been talking to my brothers."

She nodded. "Is that okay?"

He nodded. "Yes, that is what I was hoping for. Please, though, leave some time for me." He winked and stood.

She had half a mind to reach for him and yank him into the pool. "Where can I find you later?"

He grinned. "My office. Come find me and we'll talk."

She nodded and remained in the pool.

Jared clapped Aidan on the shoulder. "I prefer you remove your clothes before jumping in my pool, but I can already tell you may tell me to fuck off with that."

"You say you can't read minds," Aidan teased. "But you heard me loud and clear. Fuck off, my brother."

Jared chuckled and left the pool area, leaving Olivia alone with her sensual, chocolate skinned man. His golden eyes stared into hers.

He smirked. "May I join you?"

Chapter Eight

IT HAS BEEN considered rude to stare and drool at something delicious. However, Olivia stared at Aidan as he removed his clothes and was grateful for being wet in the pool. It would hide any evidence of her drooling.

He unbuttoned his button-down shirt and slid it off his arms. He wore an undershirt tank that hugged his body in the most delectable way. He removed his pants and stood in his tank and boxer briefs. He then removed his tank.

Oh holy shit, is he going to get completely naked?

Aidan walked to the edge of the pool, then dove in. Graceful under the water, he swam toward her. He came up and wiped his face with his hand.

"Hello, beautiful," he said. His smile put his fangs on appearance. "Have you enjoyed yourself so far?"

She did not answer immediately, giving consideration to her answer. She stared into his golden eyes. Had she enjoyed herself? Sure. Was it pleasant? Yes. Was she happy, though? She wasn't quite sure.

"Hmm, I like a woman who has to think about her answer instead of popping something off," he told her.

Olivia gave a crooked smile. "Honestly, it's a hard question to answer."

"Oh?" he asked and rested his arm on the side of the pool. "Has something happened to make you think this was not a good pairing?"

She shook her head. "No, not in the least. I think," She paused for a moment, then continued. "Let me see how I can word this."

"Don't think, just speak," he told her.

She nodded. "I was born into this life. This is not something I would have chosen for myself. My right to have free will was taken from me the moment I was conceived. My life belongs to you five, now. I have no choices in what I do from this point forward."

"Is that what you think?" he asked.

"Is that not the truth?"

He shook his head. "No, not at all. Yes, you're under a conditional agreement, however, you are not a slave to this home, or to us. You are welcome to leave if you're not happy, but you will be paired to someone else."

Victor crossed her mind and she shifted her gaze toward the other side of the pool. "I know that. I appreciate what I have here, please know that." She turned back to him. "My life turned around and upside down the morning I woke to my pairing. I walked in expecting to be paired to one vampire, and instead, I have five."

"Yeah, baby, you hit the jackpot, didn't you?" He grinned and moved in closer toward her.

She laughed and shook her head. "Yeah, you could definitely say that. Everyone has been so nice, patient, and no one has tried to force me into anything."

"Well, that's good," he said. "I'm not a fan of rape or the rape culture, myself."

Her eyes widened. "Ohmigosh," she blurted. "That is not what I meant."

He chuckled. "I know, baby girl, I know."

She lifted her brow. "Baby girl?"

He nodded. "Is that okay, if I call you baby girl?"

Her smile slipped into something of her own version of a Cheshire grin. Then, she nodded. "Yeah, I like it." She wondered about Aidan's background and where he came from. The stories she'd heard so far, everyone had been involved, one way or the other. "Aidan, would you mind sharing your story with me?"

He nodded. "Absolutely. I met Ethan almost one hundred years ago. I was already a vampire. He introduced me to Jared, and the rest is history."

Olivia waited for more, but when he did not offer, she pushed. "That can't be all."

"It's not." Aidan lowered his gaze and a vulnerability overcame him. "Ethan found me at the lowest point in my undead life."

She rested her hand on his arm. When he met her gaze, she smiled in hopes he would continue. Aidan returned her smile, then looked past her, as if he were looking into his own history.

"I had been paired shortly after being turned. My maker did not stick around to see me through. I was a bit reckless, but my lady helped me through the change and getting accustomed to my new life."

"Your lady?" Olivia asked.

He nodded. "My concubine."

She raised her brows. Of course, they have had other concubines in their existence. She would not be their first. Definitely not their last.

"We were together for a long time," he continued. "Her name was Maxine. She was everything to me. I never mated with anyone and took her as mine. We were happy. Then, one day, I came home to an empty house, or so I thought until I came upon her body in the kitchen."

Olivia gasped. "Aidan, you don't—"

He continued on. "She was murdered. A part of me died with her that day. I fell into a darkness I never want to venture into again. Ethan found me soon after and he, along with Jared and the others, saved me from myself."

"Oh, Aidan," she whispered. "I'm so sorry." She cupped his cheek and leaned in, pressing a soft kiss to his forehead. "I didn't know."

He nodded and met her gaze. It was as if he switched off the past and turned the present back on. "Well, you're here now, and we're all looking forward to next steps."

She grinned. Pushing his story to the back of her mind, she felt a new kinship with Aidan. "Me, too."

Aidan stalked her even closer. "Good. Because we plan on making you scream our names."

Her body shook and her breath came out in a rasp. "Aidan," she whispered.

"Yeah, baby girl?" he asked and reached for her. He slipped an arm around her waist and pulled her against his body.

She wrapped her arms around his neck. Olivia became fixated on his lips, his fangs seeming to grow the longer she stared. "I've never been with more than one man at a time."

He grinned. "Then, I'm looking forward to giving you another first."

"Another first?" she asked, then realized what he meant. There were few times as an adult one would have a 'first experience' on anything. This would be a first experience Olivia would never forget. And, if she were lucky, they would remind her of this experience over and over again.

"Oh," he whispered. "What's on your mind? You just blushed a red so bright, it makes me feel dirty to imagine your naughty thoughts."

She laughed out loud and relaxed in his embrace. "I was thinking how it would feel, to have all five of you feeding from me at once."

He repositioned them to where her back rested against the pool. "I need to steal a kiss. I feel I cannot breathe properly unless I have felt your lips on mine."

"That has to be the sexiest, sweetest thing—" She was cut off when his lips claimed hers. Olivia opened her mouth for him and his tongue teased hers in an erotic, suggestive, arousing way. She moved her legs to wrap them around his waist.

Unless he removed his boxer briefs, and she removed her bathing suit bottoms, there was no chance of penetration, but it would not stop any teasing, titillation from occurring. She was on the crest of masturbating in the pool, but now, with Aidan between her legs, she rubbed his rock-hard cock against her throbbing clit.

She gasped and her head lolled back. Aidan took advantage ofher exposed neckline. Fear reminded her she was in the arms of a vampire, but trust she had acquired since being in this home told her he was safe.

He caressed her neck with anticipated eagerness, the need for blood clearly intense, but giving into what she longed for instead; a much-needed release. Aidan gripped a handful of her hair and pulled hard. She gasped as he nibbled on her earlobe. His body moved with hers, causing friction between them. Her clit responded with a massive throb and she moaned, her voice echoing in the pool's chamber.

"Aidan," she whispered. "You're going to make me come."

"Mmm," he groaned into her neck. "Give it to me, baby girl. Give it all to me."

She gripped his shoulders. Giving into the moment, she opened her legs wider as his cock rubbed against her throbbing clit. The sexual frustration that had built over the last few days culminated in this moment. The orgasm rushed through her body and she yelled out. Her body shook and she rode out the wave of sensations. She came hard, warm, and yelled out his name.

Aidan slowed down and released the grip on her hair. He brushed his lips across hers in a gentle, loving way. He held her close to his body, massaging her back. "Are you all right?" he whispered.

She nodded and rested her forehead against his shoulder. "I will be." She laughed and shook her head. "I can't believe we just did that."

"Well, if I may be so bold, I cannot wait for the real thing. I'm looking forward to the day we claim you, all five of us."

She fidgeted for a moment and bit her lip. "I am, too," she whispered. "I'm also scared to death about five sets of fangs in my skin."

He chuckled.

She looked at him and frowned. "Why is that funny?"

"Baby girl," he said. "I'm not laughing at you. What I found humorous is five dicks pointing at you gives you no fear."

"I don't even know what to say that." She laughed.

"Come on, let's get showered and cleaned up." Aidan climb out of the pool and when he turned to face Olivia, his cock was at full attention.

Good lord, he's huge. She stared at him, at least until Aidan chuckled.

"Take my hand, baby girl. You can ogle my dick later."

She gasped andher eyes widened. "I wasn't..." she paused, then laughed. "Yeah, I was. I won't lie. I ogled you, as you said, like the cartoon wolf, tongue and all."

He bent down, offering his hand for her, and she grasped it. He pecked her on the cheek, then patted her butt. "I'll see you later, then."

"Yeah, I'm looking forward to it." Olivia watched Aidan as he jogged out of the pool area, disappearing behind doors. She sighed and laughed to herself. She had an orgasm in the pool by friction.

What would it be like with all five of them on me?

Holy hell, they will ruin me, in the best possible way.

She grabbed a towel and wrapped it around her, then headed to the showers. She thought about Aidan's story. He lost what he considered to be his mate. Was it the love of his life? Maybe, but with the eternal life of a vampire, Maxine would not be the last.

Next on her list was Jared, but first, she needed a moment to herself. She would raid the kitchen for baking goods and see what she may be able to create. She needed to bake, and figuring out what each man meant to her in terms of flavor would be just the thing to do.

Chapter Nine

WHEN OLIVIA CONSIDERED becoming a pastry chef, she knew there would be occasions of making cupcakes, wild cakes, and oddly shaped wedding cakes. As she stood in her new gourmet style kitchen, she pulled the straps of an apron around her body and tied it. The white material had cotton type lace around the edge of it. It reminded her of something someone's grandmother would wear. She found it cute.

She lost track of time and the world she was in when she baked. Today was no exception. She had spent time with everyone, except Jared, but he would definitely be soon. Considering him the leader of her stable, she found him fitting a red velvet cupcake. Atop it, cream cheese ice cream with a chocolate ganache colored blood red. She tilted her head as she inspected her dessert and grinned.

"Perfect," Olivia whispered.

"Ooh, that looks so yummy!"

Turning toward the kitchen entrance, a woman stepped in she did not recognize. Tall and medium build, sandy blonde hair, and a smile that instantly drew one in as a friend.

"Hello," Olivia said and moved toward her. "Who are you?"

"I'm Megan, concubine to the vampires Enzo and Malcom." Megan held her hand out for Olivia.

Olivia wiped her hand on her apron then shook Megan's hand. "It's very nice to meet you. Are your friends here as well?"

Megan nodded. "Jared called Enzo and asked us to make a stop by. I think they wanted you and I to meet. You know, concubine to concubine."

Olivia smirked. "Well, you're just in time, then." She motioned to a barstool for Megan to sit. "I don't mind you watching, but baking, I prefer to work alone. I get in my zone, you know?"

"Totally," Megan told her and took a seat. "So...five vampires?"

That didn't take long.

"Yeah, I didn't know coming into this." She shifted her gaze up at Megan and smirked, then picked up a blond coconut cupcake. She piped caramel icing on it, then topped it with crunchy coconut. She crossed her arms over her chest and eyed the cupcake for a moment, then nodded.

"Are you making a cupcake for each guy?"

Olivia grinned and nodded. "It helps get me out of my head, if just for a while."

"I read to do that. Then, when my guys need to feed, it generally takes them a few hours."

Olivia raised her brows and mouth opened in surprise. "Hours? For two to feed on you?"

Megan grinned and raised a wicked brow. "Oh no, honey, the feeding is merely moments. It's the sex that follows that is mind-blowing and takes hours."

Olivia closed her mouth and swallowed the lump that formed in her throat.

Hours?

Five of them?

How can I do that?

Can my body sustain for five?

It would be like a damn marathon!

Megan giggled. "Honey, they wouldn't push all five dongs in you at once."

Olivia laughed out loud. "Did you seriously just say *dong*?"

Megan shrugged. "Yep. Sure did." She winked at Olivia. "You know they would not expect you to take them on all at once."

Olivia shook her head and picked up her next cupcake, a peach flavored one. She grabbed the piping bag with cinnamon icing and smeared it over the top. She sat it down and laid a few jellied peach candies she made prior to the baking marathon. She put one on top of the cupcake, handed one to Megan, then popped one in her mouth. She nodded at her work so far.

"So far, who do we have?" Megan asked.

Olivia pointed to the red velvet. "Jared. The coconut is Ethan. This peach one is Jake. I made a blood orange dreamsickle for Landon, and peanut butter cheesecake that I stuffed with brownie ice cream for Aidan."

"Umm, where is the last one? I need this in my life." Megan chuckled.

Olivia laughed with her and put the other two cupcakes on display, topped them, and pushed them in front of Megan.

"My men...in cake form."

Megan ran her finger through the peanut butter cheesecake and licked it off. "It's so good. You have a gift."

"Thank you," Olivia said. "Too bad the guys wouldn't enjoy eating them."

"You know, if you offered, they would eat them because you made them."

Olivia smiled. "As sweet as the sentiment would be, they still would not enjoy it. I imagine it would be like eating dirt rather than having blood."

Megan wrinkled her nose. "Nasty."

Olivia took off her apron and walked around the counter and sat down next to Megan. "I do have some questions."

Megan nodded and shifted on her seat to face her. "Fire away."

"How long have you been their concubine?"

"Umm, going on five years," she told her.

"Weren't you scared going in?" Olivia asked.

She shook her head no. "Not at all. I was prepared for this after I became a teenager. My mom understood what my life was meant for. She was setup to enjoy her life once I was paired."

"Whoa, they bought her silence?" Olivia asked.

Megan smirked and shook her head. "No, not quite. Each Incubus is registered with the coven. In order for the vampires to continue living, they require a blood demon." She pointed between the two of them. "Case in point."

Olivia nodded. "So, there's a chance I could find out who impregnated my mother?"

Megan shrugged. "Possibly. Most pregnancies are documented when the Incubus reports who they slept with. But, I'll be honest, the records are so convoluted it's hard to know who fucked who and who parented who."

Olivia sat back a little. Disgust overcame her and she sneered. "I don't really want to think about who slept with my mom. I'd just like to know, maybe, who my father was."

"Did they have the information at your pairing?"

Olivia shook her head no. "Unfortunately not. Everything was so rushed, I didn't get a chance to even ask. I kind of felt like a fish looking out from the bowl. So many wanted to buy me and take me home, but only one lucky person could win the goldfish."

"Weird analogy, but I get it. I still remember my pairing. Enzo was there and offered me his hand. I took it and the next day, I found out about Malcolm. At least you knew going in."

Olivia snorted. "No, I actually didn't. Jared offered his hand and the other four surrounded us. I had no idea until it was already done."

Megan shook her head with a sly smile. "Damn, girl, to be in the middle of all that hotness!"

Olivia felt herself blush and she folded her hands on the countertop. "I've only spent one on one time with them. Well, not yet with Jared, but he's next." She glanced at Megan, then leaned in. In a whisper, she asked, "Does it hurt?"

"Does what hurt? The bite or the sex?"

Olivia shrugged. "Both, I suppose. I mean, I've had sex, but not with a vampire. They tell me it won't hurt when they bite, but I'm scared of needles. I look at them and see ten needles waiting to penetrate my skin. My heart beats all wild and I feel anxiety shoot through my veins." She shook her head. "I don't know what to do to get out of my own head."

Megan reached for Olivia's hand, giving it a small squeeze. "Honey, it doesn't hurt. Before they bite, they will lick your skin. Something in their saliva will numb your skin. So, when they bite? No pain. Actually, it's quite erotic, if I may say so myself."

Olivia raised her brows. "Really?"

Megan nodded. "You know how it feels when they kiss your neck, lick your nipple? Suck on your earlobe? It's hot, right?" Olivia nodded and bit her lip. "Well? It's like that, but a hundred times more! The sensations are out of this world incredible! They will give you the most extreme orgasm you have ever experienced, and that's before sex!"

Olivia thought back to the pool with Aidan.

Is Megan right?

Am I holding out because I'm scared?

"There is another option, though you may not like it."

"What's that?" Olivia asked.

"They can bring in a volunteer. When a concubine loses her vampire, they are basically like a heroin addict. Once they've tasted their vampire's blood, it is hard to be released back into general public. It's cruel. So, they are brought to the coven to live out their lives as volunteers. When vampires need a fix before they're paired, these volunteers are offered up. However, now that they have you, they have no need for a volunteer, but if they don't feed soon, they won't have much of a choice."

Considering this, Olivia placed her hands in her lap. She had options outside of giving her blood to her stable. She could bite the bullet, so to speak, and allow them to feed on her, or have them bring in a volunteer and she watch what occurs.

"I may want to watch the first time, so I know what I'm in for," Olivia said.

Megan raised her brows. "Are you positive?"

Olivia nodded. "Yeah, why?"

"Well," Megan started and her voice pitched a little higher on the end of her word. "You may be shocked at how you react once you see them feed on another blood demon."

"What, like jealousy?"

"Something like that. Maybe more like territorial."

She shook her head. "No, I don't think so. I mean, we've not shared anything yet." She felt like everything she had learned so far was thrown away. She sighed and tried again. "Let me clarify. We have shared stories, a few stolen kisses, some pool time," she blushed.

Megan giggled. "It doesn't take much of their touch to bring you to orgasm."

She grinned and waved off the statement. "We'll see. I'd like to have a volunteer come in first so I can see what happens."

"Well, I'll make sure Jared is ready to catch you when you fall."

Olivia frowned. "What's that supposed to mean?"

Megan grinned. "You'll see."

***

The doorbell rang and Olivia took a seat in a chair Jared had brought out for her. She was setup in the fountain room and she crossed her legs. Landon walked into the room with a woman who had the appearance of a *Cosmo* magazine model.

Her hair was blonde, pulled into a messy bun. Her makeup was applied lightly and she sported sunglasses on her face. She was tall and slender. She wore a black cocktail dress fitted to her body.

Olivia felt a little taken aback. When she heard these volunteers were addicted to blood, she assumed someone who looked like they were pulled off the street dirty would enter their home. Instead, in came *Audrey Hepburn*, incarnate.

The woman pulled off her glasses and whispered something to Landon, and he smiled at her. She took a seat a few feet from Olivia. The woman nodded at her and held out her hand.

"Hi, my name is Candace. Nice to meet you."

Olivia looked at her hand, expecting to see marks from fangs up and down her bare arm, but only saw smooth skin. She shook the woman's hand. "Olivia. Nice to meet you."

"So, you're new to all this?"

Olivia nodded then crossed her arms over her chest. She began to grow uncomfortable with this situation. Was Megan right, or did she place false thoughts in her head?

Landon stood to the side of Candace. He winked at Olivia and she winked back at him. A moment later, Jared, Jake, Ethan, and Aidan walked into the open area. The room was silent except for the sound of the water in the fountain, and Olivia's heartbeat. It thumped in her head and sped up the moment the rest of her men joined the room.

Her men.

Her stable.

Mine.

Candace situated herself in her seat and appeared to be overcome with joy. Olivia stared at the woman before her and found her first flaw; her eyes were dark and sunken. Olivia raised her brows to this. Maybe she really was an addict. Candace then raised her arms in the air. Landon took one, Jake the other. Jared moved behind her and tilted her head to the side. Aidan kneeled in front of her and Ethan kneeled at her side.

Jared bent down and his lips parted barely a breaths distance from Candace. Then, his gaze made contact with Olivia.

A rumble vibrated in Olivia and she realized she was growling.

Aidan pushed Candace's legs apart and licked up the inside of her thigh.

Landon licked her inner arm. Jake the same on the other.

Olivia's body shook. She fisted her hands and closed her eyes.

"No," came a heavy, thick voice. "You will watch and not close your eyes."

Olivia opened her eyes at Jared. He fisted the woman's hair in his hands and she moaned in anticipation. Not one of the vampires had penetrated her skin.

Defiant, Olivia huffed and looked the other way.

Another growl filled the air and as if it were a threat, Olivia stood and growled back, but louder. She stalked across the floor toward her stable of men. She held Jared's gaze and did not waver. As Landon lifted Candace's arm to bite, Olivia slapped her hand over the woman's arm.

"No." She then shifted her stare to Landon. "Mine." She did the same to Jake. Both men took a step back and they smirked.

Olivia grabbed Aidan by his shoulder and pushed him back, then moved herself in between him and Candace. Ethan had already backed away the moment she approached.

She then caught Candace's manic gaze. It was filled with need. She also had tears in her eyes.

"Please," the woman whispered.

The glamour, the makeup, all of it wore through and the real addict surfaced.

"Please!" Candace screamed. Her voice echoed through the home.

Olivia shifted her gaze up to Jared once more. "Release her," she said in a low voice. "Now."

Jared grinned and let go of Candace's hair. He took a step back and the woman cried out. She took a swipe at Olivia, but she was too fast. Olivia caught her arm and shoved it away. She then grabbed Candace by her cheeks and came down to her, nose to nose.

"This is *my* house. This is *my* stable. These are *my* stallions. You will leave before I ruin you forever. Get out of my house. *Now.*"

Candace quickly got to her feet and sobbed. She wiped at her eyes and shook her head. "I lost my vampire. I have nothing!"

Olivia took a few steps toward her. A part of her felt sorry for the woman, but the rest of her wanted to hurt her. If an addict takes claim on something that is not theirs, you may never get it back. Olivia staking her claim on her men secured that for her. She reached for Candace and squeezed her arms, gently.

"You need to get help. I bet there are programs—"

"Programs for who? Blood demons who are now nothing but blood whores? Right." She turned away and pushed Olivia's hands away. "My ride is outside." Candace looked over her shoulder and sneered. "Pray I never see you in public."

Olivia growled and watched the woman disappear out the door. When it closed behind her, Olivia inhaled a deep breath, then slowly exhaled.

Until she heard a chorus of growls behind her.

Turning around in a slow movement, all five men were lined up shoulder to shoulder. Jared in the middle, flanked by his four brothers.

Her stable.

Mine.

Olivia smirked and any fear she had prior faded away. She wanted her men. She needed to feel their hands on her body. A predatorial desire surged through her body to claim her men, and for them to claim her.

She took a few strides across the floor until she stood in front of Jared. She then looked at the men on his right, then his left. You could hear a pin hit the floor.

"I'm sorry I cost your dinner for you tonight," she whispered.

"We need to feed," Jared told her, his voice gravelly with desire. He reached for her and cupped the side of her head.

She leaned her face into his hand and closed her eyes. Her lips parted and she exhaled softly. "Then, let me feed you."

"No."

She opened her eyes. "What?"

"You're not ready," he told her. He let a finger glide over her cheek, down her neck, over the outline of her breast. She shivered at his touch. Jared leaned in and tilted her head up, then captured her in a kiss. He seduced her lips and with a swipe of his tongue, her mouth opened for him.

Then, he ended it. "I need you, we need you, but we need you willing and ready. Not a predator stalking her prey."

"What?" she pulled away from him.

Jared gripped her by the back of the neck and pulled her back against him. "Don't think we did not hear you growl, hear the dominance in your voice, hear you call us yours. We heard you, loud and clear."

"Then, let me feed you, please."

"Not. Yet."

She could hear the struggle in his voice. She felt a sense of rejection overwhelm her and she sagged, then nodded.

"Meet me in my office. You and I will talk," Jared told her. He released the hold on her neck and stepped past her. The other men stared at her for a moment, then all four went their own ways.

Olivia was left alone in the room with the fountain. She sobbed and fell to her knees.

What had just happened? She wanted them and they wanted her. Then, they walk away from her. She was ready for them.

Am I ready?

Yes, I know I'm ready.

I can do this. I need to do this.

She wiped her face and sniffed a few times, then got back to her feet. Her legs buckled but she caught herself. She knew where Jared's office was. This would either end now and she would be released, or things would progress very quickly after their talk.

She held onto the hope for the latter.

Chapter Ten

ANXIETY.

Fear.

Anger.

No, rage. Yes, all rage.

Olivia made her way toward Jared's office to 'talk'. The further she walked, the more the rage consumed her. She was like a kettle on a stove. Her body held the vapor and trying to compress it, it would soon explode into a fit of screams, like a banshee. If she did not allow the steam to escape, she would annihilate anything around her.

While her heels struck the tiled floor, she caught her reflection as she passed a mirror. She stopped and back stepped to look at herself.

Her hair was down around her shoulders, slightly disheveled from Jared's manhandling. She closed her eyes as she held onto that image. He did not scare her. In fact, she longed for him to do it again while he fed from her.

Needles scared her, but teeth...fangs were different. She had an urge to submit to these men and allow all of them to take what they needed, including her body. She glanced at herself again. She'd arrived a vulnerable woman unaware of the confines behind closed doors that consumed a blood demon's life. Now, fully aware of what she was in for, she was ready to give herself to her stable, completely.

She smoothed her hair down with her hands, wiped the residue of spilled tears and eyeliner from underneath her eyes, and pulled out her tube of red lipstick. She slid the crimson across her lips, then tucked the tube back into her pocket. She raised a single brow and called upon the confidence deep inside her. She knew it was there. It was finding the confidence, holding on to it, and never letting it go.

Olivia turned her head to the left and studied the hallway. At the end was Jared's office. At the end would be the determining factor of if she stayed, or if she would be asked to leave. If she had any say in the matter, she would not only stay, she would claim her stable.

"Mine," she whispered and began her descent down the corridor.

Five men.

Five different personalities.

Five sets of fangs.

Ten teeth punching through her skin.

Five cocks penetrating her.

Her body shivered in delight at these thoughts. To be seduced by one man, maybe two, was nice. It was fun. It was a sprint. Hurry up and finish sprint, get ready for the next one. But to be seduced, teased, tasted, fed on, fall in love with, and have sex with five different men, all in the same sitting, if not at the same time, was a marathon she was eager to begin.

The further down the hall she stepped, the louder her shoes struck the tile. It was the pivotal moment in a movie where the victim turned into the heroine. Everything became louder, clearer, and every movement became slower. Like stepping through molasses that seeped over your feet.

Olivia stopped in front of Jared's closed office door. On the other side sat her future, her fate, her destiny. She closed her eyes and sent up a silent prayer she would walk in and be heard. Opening her eyes one more, she grit her teeth.

I hope he hears me out and knows I want this as much as they do.

Please, don't push me away again.

She wrapped her hand around the handle and hesitated.

I should knock.

She let go of the handle and raised her fist to the door. She again hesitated.

A strong woman would just walk in and stake her claim. I should be a strong woman like this. Kick down his fucking door and demand he understand they are mine. No one else's. He'll fall to his knees and beg me for forgiveness.

Then she snorted at her own musings.

Jesus, Liv, just fucking knock already.

She closed her eyes and sucked in a deep breath, then knocked on the door.

"Enter," Jared called from the other side.

Olivia grasped the doorknob once more, gave it a turn, and pushed the door open. She stepped inside and with a few steps, paused in the middle of the room. Before her, a wooden desk and behind it, Jared sat and typed a few keys. Behind him on the wall hung a portrait of all five men in suits. Jared in the middle, flanked by Ethan and Jake, then Landon and Aidan. It was exquisite. Each male in a tuxedo, hands folded in front of their bodies, all smirking in their own way. She pictured herself in a chair in front of them.

Her stable.

Mine.

She turned her gaze and a statue of an angel rested upon a cabinet. Her wings were expanded as she held her hands in front of her. Olivia shifted her gaze back at Jared and found him watching her.

"Close the door," he ordered.

She turned toward the door and pushed it closed until the latch clicked. Her hands on the frame, she lowered her head slightly and closed her eyes. Olivia was at a loss for words. As strong as she wanted to be walking in, she now felt like a dormouse.

Do I turn to face him?

Will he address me first?

She gritted her teeth.

Grow some fucking balls, Liv.

Before she could turn to face Jared, a force pressed against her, capturing her, pinning her to the door. Her eyes opened with a start. Her wrists were held above her head and a foot kicked her legs apart. A chill fanned across her neck when Jared spoke next to her ear.

"Is this what you want?" he growled, menacing.

She exhaled and rather than fear, adrenaline spiked. She did not freeze or fight back. She allowed Jared to hold her against the door. He may be holding her, but she was in control. All she had to do was say stop, and he would. He would not hurt her. He would have earlier in front of his brothers if that were the case.

"Yes," she whispered.

"What? I can't hear you. If this is what you want, you need to tell me. Right now, Olivia, or it's all over."

"Fuck, yes, this is what I want!" she growled at him. "Why do you think I'm in here? I want you! All of you!"

Jared did not relent. He held her against the door, tightening his grasp on her wrists. With the other, he pushed it around her waist, down between her legs. He pressed a finger against her panties, teasing her clit. Breath fanned across her neck and he flicked her ear with his tongue. Using his tongue, he licked up the side of her neck and pressed his finger harder against her clit. He then pressed his pelvis against her ass.

She groaned and her head lolled back. She could feel his erection. He was in need for more than a simple feeding. Candace had been provided as sustenance and Olivia had sent her away. Now, she presented herself as his next meal and she needed so much more.

He pushed past the material of her panties and rubbed her clit. It throbbed for release and her pussy longed to take his cock deep inside her. He pressed against the swollen bud and moved his fingers back and forth in a quick, furious movement.

Olivia gasped and her legs buckled. "Oh my God," she whispered and as she came on his hand, the cream slicked down the inside of her thighs.

"Do you want us to claim your body?" Jared snarled in her ear.

"Oh, yes, my gods, yes!"

He shoved a finger inside her pussy and hooked it against her sensitive spot. "Do you want us to feed from you, then fuck you?"

She gasped once more and her body shook. She was going to experience an orgasm that may cause her to scream out. "I just... I need... Oh my gods, Jared, please don't stop!" She could not control a thought, her breath, anything while he possessed her body.

"Tell me," he growled. "Tell me, what is your purpose here."

Her breath hitched and she pushed against the door, pressing her body harder against Jared's. She tilted her ass toward him, wanting to feel his cock against her ass. "I am here for you. I am yours."

"And?" he whispered.

"What?" she asked and screamed out. "Oh, hell, I'm going come, shit!"

Then, without warning, Jared removed his fingers. He pressed her back against the door. Olivia tried to move, but he kept a firm grip.

"What are you doing?" she asked. "Please, I'm so close. My clit is throbbing. Please, please!"

"And?" he whispered next to her ear. "Tell me and I'll make you not only come for me, but for my brothers. Tell me, now."

She yelled out and rage consumed her. He brought her to the edge just to toy with her?

Hell to the fuck no!

She pushed against him, thrashing her body. But it was like fighting a stone wall. Jared would not move.

"Dammit!" she yelled out. "What is it you're expecting me to say?"

"You already said it," he told her and nibbled her ear. She groaned and pressed her legs together. "Oh no you don't," he said and pushed her legs back apart. "You don't get to make yourself get off. You will only enjoy ecstasy once you tell me, admit to me, what your darkest desire is. I already know, but I need to hear you accept it."

"Dammit, Jared," she yelled out. "I am yours! Fucking yours!"

"And?"

"Fuck! What do you want?" She yelled and tried once more to move, to no avail. "Let me the fuck go!"

"Is that what you really want?"

Her breathing came in quick pants and she closed her eyes. He was going to drive her mad. She would go to an asylum forced into insanity by never having another orgasm, living on the brink of a release she could never reach.

This must be what Dante's Inferno second level of lust must be like. Reaching orgasm, but never having it.

Forever in a state of masturbation.

Olivia forced herself to calm, made herself think about what Jared was asking of her.

Candace came and Olivia made her leave.

She claimed the men were hers.

Mine.

She gasped. She knew the answer. Olivia opened her eyes and tried to face Jared. He would not allow her to move. She groaned.

"Please, let me face you."

He gave her this. He allowed her to turn, but kept her hands above her head. He pushed against her, shoving his leg in between hers. She wanted to grind her pussy on his thigh.

His forehead rested against hers. He was as tormented as she was. His breathing became erratic like hers. His cock pressed into her hip and she wanted so desperately to grasp the length and stroke him, suck him, fuck him.

She stared at his lips, then studied his face. He appeared to be in pain. Was he hurting? Of course he was. Here she was, in front of him, like a big juicy steak and he could not even lick her.

"Mine," she whispered.

He met her gaze. "Again, but louder."

"Mine," she spoke up.

"No, louder. Own it. Claim it. Now."

"Fuck you! You, all of you, all five of you are my stallions! You are my stable! YOU ARE MINE!" She yelled out the final words and Jared crushed his lips to hers and shoved his fingers roughly onto her clit. The nerves thrummed as Jared stroked her faster and faster. His finger slipped inside her, collected her moisture, then came out and rubbed her clit even harder.

Her thighs wet with her cream, Olivia lifted a leg around his waist. "I need you inside me." She groaned and held onto his shoulders.

Jared picked her up and carried her to his desk. Laying her down, he ran his hands up the length of her legs, then hooked his fingers over the edge of her panties. Giving them a tug, he pulled her panties down her legs, then tossed them over his shoulder. He pushed her thighs apart and smirked.

"Beautiful," he whispered. Jared began to unbutton his shirt and lowered himself into a chair. He moved himself closer to her, and grabbing her thighs, he pulled her to the edge of the desk. His fingers pulled her pussy lips apart and he growled.

Olivia reached above her head and gripped the desk. Then, Jared claimed her pussy. His mouth covered her lips and he ran his tongue from ass to clit. He sucked on her bundle of nerves and thrashed it with his tongue.

She cried out as her body shook, an orgasm promising to make an entrance soon. Letting go of the desk, she reached for Jared and tangled her hands in his hair. She pulled him closer, harder against her. Her hips moved against his mouth, gaining more friction.

He took her hands in his, pulling them away from where she gripped his head, then he let her go, and stood.

She lifted her head and watched him, panting. "Why did you stop?" She sat up and her dress fell down around her waist.

He smirked and crossed the room to the door, then opened it.

She started to reach for the edge of her clothes to remove them, but stopped when the door opened completely. On the other side were the rest of her men. One by one, they entered the room. All of them in their white button-down shirts and black pants, just like Jared. Jared removed his shirt and let it fall to the floor.

Jake stood next to him and bent down to one knee. Landon did the same next to Jake. On the other side of Jared, Ethan took a knee, Aidan next to him.

Olivia sat on Jared's desk with her stable of men before her. She met Jared's gaze once more, and the man, like his brothers, took a knee. She wasn't sure what to say or do.

Yes, she did know. She smirked and pulled her dress off over her head. She dropped it to the floor, then removed her bra. She sat naked, but not once did she feel exposed. Her men were giving themselves to her, as she offered herself to them.

She crossed one leg over the other, her thighs wet with honey from her pussy. All she had left on were her heels.

Left to right, Landon, Ethan, Jared, Jake, and Aidan. She held her hands out on either side of her body. Landon and Aidan both grasped a hand and pressed their lips to the back of each. They let her go and she offered her hands to Jake and Ethan. Like the former, they pressed a kiss to her hand. She then looked at Jared.

Rather than offering her hands to him, she curled a finger, indicating he should stand. He obeyed, stood, and approached her. She ran her hands up his naked torso, around his sides, then cupped his ass. She separated her legs and pulled him in between them, then feathered her mouth over his chest.

"Mine. All of you. *Mine.*"

Jared moved his hand to the back of her head and cradled it. He grasped her hair in his fist, tilted her head back, and slanted his mouth across hers. He guided her back down to the desk, trailing kisses down her neck, to her breasts. He cupped both pale mounds and pushed them together, sucking one nipple, then the other.

She heard a groan from one of the men. "Jake," she whispered his name. "Come to me."

Hearing movement from the floor, she opened her eyes and found Jake as he walked around the desk and stood next to her head. She reached for him and he bent down. She pulled him to her and he tilted his head, pressing his lips upon hers.

Jared moved down her body to her stomach and licked down to her naval.

"Ethan," she whispered. She offered her arm to Jake and he licked the inside of her wrist, then pressed his lips to it.

Ethan came around the desk. He grasped her cheeks, tilted her head toward him, and then stroked his tongue over the seam of her lips.

She gasped when Jared buried his face in her pussy, licking and sucking her clit. "Oh God," she whispered and lifted her other arm to Ethan.

"Landon," she called. Her back arched and she moaned. Her men holding her arms peppered their lips down her arms to her breasts. Ethan on one, Jake on the other. She felt like her body would explode in a combustion of fire.

Jared sucked on her clit and she yelled out as an orgasm rocked her body. She pressed her heels on his shoulders and moved her pussy on his face. She wanted to reach for him and pull him closer, but her arms were busy holding onto Ethan and Jake.

Then a hand, soft and gentle, slipped around her neck and tilted her head back. Landon moved his mouth over hers, capturing her lips for a brief moment, and then peppered his way to her neck. Jake and Ethan moved back, paying close attention to her arms, and Landon knelt down, laving her neck.

"Aidan, please, come to me."

A growl erupted between her legs and Jared pushed two thick fingers inside her, thrusting them deep as he sucked and nibbled on her clit.

"Fuck," she groaned and her head lolled back.

Then, Aidan moved his lips over her mouth, his hand cupping her breast, pinching the nipple. He moved to the other side of her neck, nibbling at the soft skin covering her throbbing pulse. Olivia groaned, every nerve in her body alive and on fire. She would shatter soon and when she did, there was no going back.

Jared gripped her legs and snarled against her sex. She came once more and screamed out. Then, all at once, all five stopped their kissing, their pinching, their licking, and sucking. She panted for a moment and stared at the ceiling.

Before she could ask or even think, each of them licked her; neck, arms, the inside of her thigh. All five of them hissed and Olivia closed her eyes.

No fear. Pure bliss. She relaxed in their grasps, giving over herself to her men completely. Five sets of fangs pierced her skin in unison. Five mouths suckled, drawing the life-giving elixir to the surface of her skin and gulping as her warmth flowed freely.

Power exploded inside Olivia and her body came alive with another orgasm. She moaned and her hips began to move of their own accord, bucking, begging with need. She needed someone to mount her, to fuck her, to claim her.

Jared pulled himself free first and snarled into the air. She looked down at the man and his mouth was coated in her blood. Before all of this, finding her fear on his mouth would have frightened her. Now, she loved it. Resting her head back on the table, she heard a buckle and felt a naked body pressed up against her belly. Then, the bluntness of his head pressed against her core and, without preamble, shoved inside. Her channel clamped down, welcoming the intrusion even as her body stretched to accommodate his girth.

"Oh hell, fuck yes." She groaned. Her men all released her with a snarl, a hiss, a growl. All five of her men stood above her, each with her blood coating their lips. She reached for the closest man, Landon, and pulled him to her. She fumbled with his pants and he took her hands.

"*Mi amore*," he whispered. "Allow me." He quickly removed his pants and boxers. Olivia reached for him and pulled him close. She wrapped her hand around his cock and stroked him, then pulled him to her mouth.

Landon moved his hand to the back of her head and tilted it back, cradling it.

He groaned and moved his hips back and forth, fucking her mouth.

"Fucking beautiful," Aidan whispered.

"Flip her over," Ethan said.

"Allow me," Jared said and slipped his arms underneath her body. She let go of Landon as Jared lifted her in the air. He backed up to a chair in his office and sat down with her straddling his hips, his hardness pressing into her core. Olivia moved her body against him, taking him in deeper inside her.

Behind her, Ethan pulled her hair to the side, fisting it in his hand. He caressed her and moved his mouth over her neck and shoulder. "I'm going to lube you, then fuck your ass."

"Yes," she said and tilted her head to the side. His lips captured hers and a warmth slipped down her ass, over her rear entrance. Ethan circled a finger over her hole then pushed it inside. He slipped in another finger and stretched her hole in a scissor movement. He pushed her forward toward Jared, holding her hips so tightly his fingers pressed into her flesh. There would be bruises there later, she knew. She felt his head press against her tight entrance. He gently pushed against her, breaching the tight ring of muscle and easing himself inside. She held her breath, anxious to get through the initial pain, anticipating the pleasure to come.

"Breathe, *mi amore,*" Landon whispered. "Relax, you'll be okay."

She nodded and opened her eyes to meet Landon's gaze.

"There you go, *mi amore.*" He cupped her face. He slanted his lips over hers while Ethan pushed further inside her, pausing every small inch to wait for her to accept him.

She gasped then groaned. "Holy fuck, I'm going to come, right now!"

Ethan pushed in further, then pulled back. Jared pushed in and she groaned. The two men slid back and forth in opposite motions. While one pulled, the other pushed. Sensations, nerves, everything in her body came alive. She screamed and someone licked her arm. She looked up to find Aidan sucking on her forearm. Landon pushed her hair to the side and tilted her head. He licked her neck and sunk his fangs into her once more.

Two men fucked her.

Two men sucked on her arms.

Jake.

Where was Jake?

She opened her eyes and found him watching her with a smile on his face.

She grinned. "Come feed. Let me serve you."

He smirked. "I will, while I'm inside you."

Ethan thrust inside twice more, then stilled. His head rested against hers. "Time to share," he whispered, then pressed his lips to her cheek, and pulled from her throbbing pucker.

Jared groaned and his tongue ran the length of her neck. He sucked on her earlobe. His cock still inside her. "I don't want to stop," he whispered.

"Then don't," she told him.

He growled and fucked her harder, faster. She yelled out as another orgasm slammed her, causing her back to arch.

"Brother," Jared managed to get out. "Ready yourself for this woman for she is who we have been waiting for."

Olivia met Jared's gaze and held it. She pressed her lips to his and groaned when he thrust inside her. "Allow me to taste you."

"Soon," he told her. "Once we're done, or once your body has had enough, we'll feed you and heal you."

She nodded and feathered her lips across his once more.

A set of hands grasped her shoulders and she leaned back into a strong frame. It was Jake. "Take me," she whispered.

Jared lifted her off of his body and his mouth took in one of her nipples. Her pussy was left feeling bereft, empty and wanting more. Landon and Aidan released her and she cried out her displeasure at the loss. She didn't want to stop yet.

Jake helped her stand and he cupped her face. "Are you all right?"

She nodded. "Oh, yes, I'm great, but everyone stopped." She feigned a pout.

He grinned. "Good answer. Now, turn around and bend over."

She obeyed and bent over for Jake as a thrill traced over her spine.

Jake lined up his cockhead with her back channel and, in a single thrust, pushed inside her tight ass. He groaned and grabbed her hips, thrusting hard against her. Their bodies slapped as he fucked her. Her thighs were slick with her cum, and she wanted more, needed more. He brought her to another orgasm and she braced her body on her thighs.

Olivia looked over to Aidan and her lips parted. "I need you," she whispered.

Aidan took a few steps over and stood in front of her. "Sit back, let me have that pussy."

Jake pulled his cock from her, lifted her against his chest, took a few steps back, and then sat in a chair, gently easing her down, his cock pushing back inside her ass. She took him in completely. He reached around her. "Good girl. Now, lift your legs."

She did, and Aidan pushed them toward her chest.

"Holy shit," she screamed. "Oh gods, I'm going to fucking come again, Jake! Fuck me!"

Jake thrust his body against hers, his pelvis slamming against her ass. The angle she was held shifted their position to where his head pushed against her sensitive spot.

"She's creaming, fucking creaming, man," Aidan said. He rubbed her clit and she yelled out, her body twitching.

"Fuck me," she growled.

Aidan chuckled, fit his engorged cock at the entrance to her core, then pushed inside her.

Olivia lost herself in her men. Her body exploded, orgasm after orgasm.

"We'll need to give her a rest, soon," Landon stated.

"You still need to fuck her," Jared told him.

Olivia opened her eyes and glanced over at Landon, then smirked. "Come, fuck my mouth again."

Landon groaned and mumbled something in Italian. He came to her and took her mouth with his. *"Mi amore, bella donna."* He stood, then gripped his cock and touched it to her swollen lips.

She flicked her tongue across her lips to moisten them, and then opened her mouth. Landon fisted her hair, tilted her head, and pushed his hardness in until it hit the back of her throat. She gagged and he pulled back. He did this again, then when he pulled back, he swiped the drool from her mouth and rubbed it on his cock. He pushed inside her mouth once more but allowed her to form a suction. She looked up at him as he pushed in and withdrew. He held her head as he fucked her mouth.

Olivia pulled her mouth free and stroked Landon as she screamed out. She came again and her back arched. Jake and Aidan thrust inside her faster, until Aidan yelled out with a snarl. His head tilted back and his fangs glistened in the light.

Maybe fear should have hit, seeing him like this. Instead, she smiled. Aidan looked back down at her. He moved his body against hers a few more times, then gently pulled out.

She set her legs down and Jake pulled out, then helped her stand up.

Olivia's legs suddenly gave out and she tumbled into Jared's arms. He scooped her up and pressed his lips to her forehead. She smiled at the sentiment. She relaxed in his embrace and let blackness consume her.

Chapter Eleven

IT WAS NOT every day one could claim to have experienced an out of body experience, but when Olivia opened her eyes, she felt as if she were floating. She blinked her vision from blurry to clear. Her lips twitched to form a smile. Warm, humid air floated around her. She could smell the grass as it may have been recently cut and heard the running of water.

"Sleeping beauty wakes," came the distant voice of Aidan.

Aidan.

She tilted her head in the direction of his voice and found him watching her.

"Is the water ready?" Jared asked.

Olivia turned to the man holding her. Jared met her gaze and he smirked, then something drew his attention elsewhere. She nuzzled in closer to him and sighed. She could stay like this all night. Who needed a bed?

Jared took a few steps and Olivia moved her head enough to spy where he was taking her. They were outside in what she assumed to be the backyard. From what she could see, the area was paved, each corner holding statues of women. A large cement wall in the distance gated in the yard. Just in front of them, a hot tub.

She moaned softly. "Is this for me?"

"All of this is for you," Jared whispered to her. "All of what we have, what we are, is yours."

She closed her eyes and peppered kisses along his chest to his neck. "Watch out or you'll spoil me, Jared."

"That's the plan, my love," he chuckled. "Hang on, I'm going to step in."

She nodded and intertwined her fingers around his neck. He stepped in and she could feel the heat rising up against her bare skin.

In this moment, she realized she was naked. Everyone within view would see all of her goods. Anyone who mattered in this moment was here and being exposed made her happy. Jared lowered her into the water and instant relief flooded her skin, her muscles, her body.

"How does it feel?" he asked.

"I love it," she groaned and rested her back against the wall.

"It's a salted pool. It should help with muscle ache. I assume there will be some sore spots."

She opened one eye and glared at him, playfully. "You think so?"

"I'm sure we can find out," Jake teased as he climbed in.

She shook her head with a chuckle. One by one, each of her men climbed into the hot tub. Everyone was naked during sex, but she did not get a chance at full appreciation for their bodies.

Oh, holy hell, she sure did now.

Jake had pecs and an ass you could bounce quarters off of. The man was absolutely fine. She smirked as he lowered himself.

He chuckled and nudged his brother. "Looks like someone is already feeling better, if not feisty."

Olivia's lips perked in a grin. "I'm always feisty."

Jared leaned over to her and smoothed a few hairs from her face. "Let's give her at least a few minutes before we torture her again."

Olivia laughed and shook her head. "Nothing is going in me for a few hours. Yeah, I'm sore. And, I would not consider what we did as torture."

"Well, it was worth it, right?" Ethan asked as he climbed in next. He was blond on top, as well as the bottom. He was fit, strong, and had a tattoo on his left pec. It was a half circle with zodiac signs. She made a mental note to ask him about that later.

Landon stepped in and Olivia stalked the man like a cat hunting her mouse. Her gentle artist had a wild streak in him she witnessed earlier. She recalled his cock gagging her, then had a notion of doing it again. He settled into the water and his dark curls dripped water onto his shoulders. Like his brothers, strong, chiseled, and sexy as hell. He met her gaze and winked.

That left Aidan. He had sunglasses on, who knows why as it was night time. He pulled off the look perfectly, though, and could make the top men's magazine kick themselves for not booking him. He was like a smooth piece of chocolate you wanted to suck on for hours at a time. He stepped in and sat on the other side of Olivia.

Olivia allowed her gaze to roam from Aidan to Jared, to Jake, Landon and Ethan, taking in all of her men. She grinned.

"Penny for your thoughts?" Jake asked her.

"I truly feel I have won the lottery here."

Each of them chuckled and Jared wrapped an arm around her shoulders. She leaned into him and tucked her legs under her body.

"You know," she said and looked up at him. "I heard everyone's story, but yours."

He pressed his lips on her forehead. "Not much to tell."

"Yeah, I call bullshit on that," Jake offered.

She glanced at his brother with a smile, then back at Jared. "Come on, what's your story?"

"Olivia, you don't need to hear it right now," he teased her.

"Okay, guys, please, call me Liv. Olivia is so formal. I feel we have definitely moved past formalities."

Jared shook with a chuckle and she enjoyed the deepness of his laugh. "Okay, Liv."

"Okay? You'll tell me?" She sat up with a smile. "Please?"

"I don't know what's to tell," he started. "I'm the CEO of my own company. I have a large online presence. I invest money to make money."

"That's fantastic to hear, but that's not who you are. Come on, spill!" She grinned, leaning back against the edge of the hot tub.

He sighed. "We were fighting in World War II. I lost track of Jake. I knew he was close, and also knew, eventually, we would find each other. We always did."

"Brothers thing," Jake added.

Jared nodded. "Yeah, something like that. Anyway, I was shot through the chest." He pointed to his left pec and the scar was barely visible. Olivia may not have even realized it was there unless she really looked. Even then, it did not resemble a gunshot wound.

"I was lying on my death bed," Jared continued. That evening, I had a feeling it was my last night on earth. I didn't think I'd survive the night. I began to lose consciousness, until I heard a voice. I don't know what it was about his voice, but it called to me, like a lullaby to a baby. I remember opening my eyes for the last time as a human that night. He whispered something to me about living eternal life and never falling ill again." Jared rubbed the back of his neck, then shrugged. "Who would say no to that?"

Olivia glanced over at Jake and found him staring at the spa water. She wondered if he would have chosen differently. Did Jared give him a choice?

Jared continued. "Then, the change began. The man had his arm up against my mouth and gave me no choice. I could not breathe unless I swallowed his gift, his blood."

"Wow," Olivia whispered. She glanced around at the men in the hot tub, each of them meeting her gaze. "Years later, here you all are."

"All except me," Aidan added. "I was already changed, as you know. But Jared here took me in after I lost Maxine."

She reached for Aidan's hand and squeezed it.

"Decision I've never regretted," Jared added.

Silence fell between them and Olivia pulled her knees to her chest. Tightness gripped her legs and thighs. She would need to stretch later.

The doorbell rang. She frowned and looked at Jared. "Expecting company?" she asked.

He shook his head. "No, not that I'm aware of." He moved to leave the hot tub when Aidan put his hands up.

"Nah, brother, I got it. I'll be right back." Aidan leaned over and feathered his lips over Olivia's, lowered his glasses and winked at her, then climbed out of the hot tub.

"Here, baby, give me your feet," Ethan said and reached for her. He pressed his thumbs into the souls of her feet.

She sighed a moan and lolled her head back. "Oh, yes, love this. Maybe later you can massage my sore body."

He chuckled. "Whatever you need, baby."

Their words left her mind swirling with questions she wasn't sure she should voice. They had been around at least since World War II. Each of them had a blood demon between then and now. What happened to the blood demons before her? She knew about Aidan's, but how long ago was that?

"What's going on in your head?" Jake asked. "Your mood just shifted."

"I don't know if I'll ever get used to that," she said with a chuckle. "I was thinking about who you had before me as a blood demon."

"Nothing you need to worry about," Jared told her. "Each of us had one before we formed our family."

"Yeah," Jake added. "We have been using volunteers for a while—"

"Butwe knew we needed someone that could be ours," Ethan finished.

"*Mi amore*," Landon said as he moved across the hot tub toward her. "You are the one and only for us. The only one we will ever need." He moved his fingers across her forehead, smoothing her hair back. He leaned in and brushed his lips over her forehead, down to her cheek, then across to her earlobe. "*Bella donna*," he whispered.

She leaned into his body and wrapped her arms around his neck, pulling him closer to her. She wrapped her legs around his waist and he nibbled softly on her neck.

"Hey, lover boy," Jared piped in. "Let her feed from you. Let's complete the circle."

"Feed from you?" she asked and moved her legs off of Landon's body.

"*Si*," Landon answered and brought his arm up. "No worries, *mi amore,* you will love it."

They had not lied about anything yet, why start now? Megan did tell her it was the most decadent taste she would ever experience. Now, she was curious.

"Okay," Olivia said and fiddled with her fingers. "Who will let me feed from them first?"

"Go for it," Jared told Landon.

Landon nodded and brought his arm to his mouth and bit into his flesh. Puncture holes were left from his fangs and he offered it to Olivia. "Here, *mi amore,* suck on my arm like you'd suck my cock."

She laughed and shook her head. "Not quite the same thing, but I'll try." She took his arm and blood droplets dripped into the water. His blood began to solidify on the wound. She needed to move quick. She licked her lips and sent up a silent prayer she would not gag and vomit on her men.

She took in a deep breath and leaned in. She sealed her lips over his puncture wound, as his blood pooled in her mouth. She squeezed her eyes closed, then when his warm blood hit the back of her tongue, she was pleasantly surprised.

Megan was not wrong. His blood was like the sweetest dessert, like velvet chocolate. She sucked on his arm and swallowed his blood. A moan was lured from her body. Her body awoke once more and she felt more alive in this moment than any other day in her life's existence. Everything she felt before, the soreness, pain, stiffness, immediately ceased. She felt like she could run a marathon, or another marathon of sex with her men.

She opened her eyes and everything around her appeared different, felt different. The green of the shrubs was more vibrant. The stars in the sky were brighter. The air around her, she could feel the moisture as if she were walking through a cloud.

Then her gaze landed on Jake.

"Oh, I'm next it appears," he said with a grin. He moved toward her as she released Landon. He bit into his arm and she reached for him. She licked his wound and his blood tasted similar to Landon's. Lovely and rich, she gasped as she felt his blood dribble down her chin. She wiped it off and licked her fingers.

"Fuck me, that's hot," Ethan groaned. She glanced over to him stroking his cock. She smirked.

"You're next, after Jake."

"Ahh, hell," Ethan groaned and lolled his head back.

She turned to Jake and lifted her brow.

He pointed to her mouth. "Got a little something there."

She licked her mouth and Jake made an 'ooh' with his mouth. He offered his arm to her and she greedily accepted it. Like Landon, she pulled on the wound, salivating his blood as it poured over her tongue, a more delicious decadent dessert. Her body may vibrate soon with the blood of her men.

Jake petted her head, running his hand down her back. "All right, baby, you've had enough. Ethan is ready for you."

She licked Jake's arm, met his gaze, then licked her mouth once more.

"Fuck," he whispered. "How did we get so fucking lucky?"

"Good things come to those who wait, and are fucking lucky bastards," Jared answered him.

Olivia glanced over her shoulder at Jared and smirked. "You're next, when I finish with Ethan."

"Yes, ma'am," he answered.

She turned to Ethan and straddled his body. She gripped his cock and stroked him, squeezing the head.

"Fuck, baby," he groaned. "Here, suck me and fuck me."

She grinned and took his arm after he opened a wound for her. She latched on and sucked, his blood pooling in her mouth. She held his gaze and Ethan reached between them and lined up his hardness. She slid down on his cock, his girth filling and stretching her. She anticipated pain or maybe soreness, but there was only pleasure. And it was exquisite. She rocked her hips and drank from him.

"Fuck, yes," he groaned. "Every fucking time we're doing this. Fuck, yes."

A hand fisted her hair and yanked it back. She hissed from the forced release from his arm. Jared tilted her head to the side and licked her shoulder, then bit into it.

An orgasm pulsed through her body and her body bucked. She gasped out loud and pressed herself down on Ethan harder. He reached into the water and squeezed her clit between his finger and thumb. He massaged, pinched, then rubbed it as she moved against him.

"Fuck me, holy fuck, fuck me," she whispered.

Jared released his bite and brought his arm around. She watched him bite into his flesh and when he offered it to her, she gripped it hard and slammed his arm to her mouth.

His blood, the richest, sweetest, of the four. She sucked harder and harder, feeling she would never grow full or ever have enough.

"Let her go," Jared said, and Ethan released her. "She still needs to feed from Aidan."

"Yeah, and I'm just in time!" Aidan rejoined them and Olivia opened her eyes to see him climb back into the hot tub. "What the hell did I miss?"

Jake chuckled. "Her first feeding."

"Oh," he said and moved toward her. "You loving this, baby girl? You ready for some chocolate gold?"

She did not want to release Jared, but she was curious about Aidan. And she needed his blood. Jared forced her decision by removing his arm from her mouth.

"Go on," he whispered. She turned to face Jared. She licked her lips, then pressed her mouth to his. Her tongue sought his and he moved his hands moved to her back and cupped her ass.

She embraced his body with her legs, her sex seeking his cock.

He groaned and pulled away from their kiss. "Go, before I pull you onto my cock."

"Would that be so bad?" she asked.

He chuckled. "I may take you from behind. Go."

She grinned and turned to face Aidan. She motioned for him to come to her. Olivia sat between Jared's legs, and she spread hers.

"Hold my legs for me?" she asked Jared. He obliged and hooked his hands behind her knees. "Landon?"

Landon's brows perked and he grinned. "*Mi amore*, is this for me?"

She nodded. "Come, take me while I feed from Aidan. You had my mouth, but not my body."

"Oh, *bella donna*," he whispered and moved through the water to her body. He pressed his cock to her entrance and pushed. She gasped and rested her head back on Jared.

"Aidan," she gasped and met the man's gaze. "Let me have your blood."

Aidan didn't say another word. He bit into his arm and she pulled it to her mouth. She closed her eyes and tilted her head.

She felt a tongue lick her neck and Jared move behind her. His mouth pressed to her neck and he bit into her flesh.

Aidan pinched her nipples and massaged her breasts. "Nothing finer than a beautiful woman feeding while being fucked."

With each thrust from Landon, he hit the sensitive spot inside her channel. She moaned against Aidan's arm and Jared sucked on her neck.

Jake and Ethan moved in closer. She opened her eyes to the men surrounding her and released Aidan's arm. She licked her mouth one last time, then offered her arms to her men.

Jake took her left arm, licked the forearm and then bit into her. He sat back next to his brother, leaving an open space for Ethan.

Ethan leaned in and licked her nipple, then he bit down.

Landon took her right arm and licked over the thready pulse at her wrist, then sliced his teeth into her flesh.

"I'm going to fuck your ass," Jared whispered. She nodded and Landon thrust harder inside her.

"I did not think I could do another round of this, but holy fuck, your blood...it is like magic fuel."

Jared chuckled and lifted her just enough to rub his finger over her hole. He took the head of his cock and pressed it to her entrance, then pushed.

"Oh my god, yes, yes!" she screamed. "Fuck me, please!'

"Once we're done here," Aidan groaned against her arm. "We've been called to the coven."

"To lock everything in?" Jared asked and thrust hard against her ass.

She screamed out from pain, and from an orgasm she rode out. "Fuck me, do that again!"

Jared chuckled and thrust hard against her once more.

"That's my guess," Aidan answered him then leaned into Olivia. He cradled her head and slid his lips over hers.

Olivia yelled out against his mouth as an orgasm ripped through her body, causing her to gasp out loud. Her head lolled back onto Jared and she screamed their names. "Jared! Jake! Ethan! Landon! Aidan! Holy hell, fuck me!"

Water splashed, blood from the bite wounds dripped into the hot tub, the smell of sex hung heavy in the air. She let herself go to her men and had no intentions of ever looking back.

Chapter Twelve

OLIVIA STEPPED INTO the kitchen in her red halter dress with a low skirt, and black shoes. Her dark hair pulled to the nape with a red wrap around headband. She was the epitome of pinup woman, and she loved it. She knew her men would as well.

She pulled out a few mixing bowls and considered making chocolate cupcakes with shots of her blood in vials.

Did it sound disgusting?

Absolutely.

Would her men love it?

Hell to the yes.

She opened the fridge and pulled out her eggs, milk, and spied the vials of blood she'd drawn earlier. When she closed the door, she saw a magnet on the top, the King of Hearts. She had a thought, pull the King card and the four Jacks. King Jared on top, with his four stallions. In the center of it all, the Queen of Hearts, herself.

Giggling to herself, she cracked the eggs, poured in the milk, and started to whisk. A throat clearing caught her attention. She turned to find her sexy King of Hearts stepping into the kitchen.

Jared wore a dark gray suit, white button-down shirt, and a black tie he was in the process of straightening. "Don't you look like sex on legs?" he grinned and pulled her into his arms. "I could eat you alive." His lips slanted over hers and tilted her back. He squeezed her ass in his hands. "I would lick the cakes off your body if it meant having you once more before we leave."

Her pussy heated and throbbed with need. She pressed her legs together to quench the fire he ignited. "As much as I would love you to do that, you have a meeting with the coven to go to." She tapped his nose. "I have a surprise for you five when you get home."

"Does it involve you being naked?" asked Jake when he entered the kitchen, followed by Ethan, Landon, and Aidan. Each of them wore dark suit colors and damn, she wanted to take them all to her bedroom. Whether it was feeding, fucking, or a combination of all three, she was ready for more.

All her stallions in one room.

Mine.

"Absolutely," she said and leaned her back against the counter. Palms pressed against it, a thought came to mind, something she had not considered, or even realized. The men did not have a release of their own. "Can I ask a question...maybe TMI?"

Landon chuckled. "Nothing is TMI at this point in our relationship with you, *Mi amore*."

She nodded and crossed one ankle over the other. "Do you not climax?" She raised her sight first to Jared.

Her vampire raised his brows. "In all my years as a vampire, no one has ever asked me if I experience an orgasm."

She bit her lip. "I meant no offense."

He shook his head. "None taken. Actually, I think I'm flattered you asked."

"Well," she shrugged. "I noticed no one, except me, had an orgasm."

"I would like to add in there were multiple," Jake said with a chuckle.

She felt her face and ears flush. "Yes, very true."

"It's hard to explain. We do not have orgasms in the traditional sense. Our release is being able to feed during sex. That gives us the fulfillment we desire."

"Well, that explains a lot, then."

"How's that?" Ethan asked.

"Well? No heartbeat, so no blood to pump. No orgasm. But," she paused, then frowned. "How do you get an erection?"

"It's like the feeling you get when something pokes you," Aidan answered. "Imagine a pin pricking your skin. It would hurt, right?" Olivia nodded. "It's the same concept with us. We think what we need, and bam," he used both hands to point to his nether regions. "Erection."

She raised a brow. "So, if you wanted wings, you think them and bam, they appear?"

"Smart ass," he growled, then chuckled. "No. No wings. Just on our body."

"Like insta-viagra!" she said with a smile.

Jared chuckled. "Sure, you could say that."

"All right, my loves, you should be off. When you return, I'll have dessert ready. Oh, and cupcakes," she winked.

The men chuckled, then one by one, each pulled Olivia into an embrace.

Jared pressed his lips to her forehead. "I hate to leave you alone, but we will be back before you know it."

"Don't worry about me. I have your phone, and if I get lonely, I'll give Megan a call."

He nodded. "I'm glad you made a friend. Oh, speaking of friends..." He released her and took a step back. "Sherlock is on his way."

She squealed and jumped into his arms. She brushed her lips across his forehead, cheeks, nose, and his lips.

"Thank you, thank you, thank you! Oh, I miss him so much!"

He chuckled and held her in his arms. "You're welcome. He should be here sometime today."

She let him go and clapped her hands, bouncing in her step. "Oh, I'm so excited!"

Ethan chuckled. "I can see that."

"So, how long do you think y'all will be gone?" She thought about what she would do after the cupcakes were made and decorated. Long, hot bath, maybe paint her nails, or better yet, take a nap. She'd need her energy. Maybe Sherlock would be here with her. Definitely one on one playtime with him.

Jared tugged on the sleeves under his sports coat. "I'm not sure. Aidan," he turned to his adopted brother. "Did we confirm if we're finalizing the pairing? I can't imagine what else they would need us for."

Aidan shrugged. "That's my assumption. All I got was we're needed."

Jared nodded and turned back to Olivia. "You'll be fine here alone?"

"Of course," she beamed. "I'll keep myself busy. However, it may benefit the entire house to hire help? Not that we need someone to cook—"

"You have me for that, my love," Jake added.

She smiled at him. "Well, I was going to say, someone like Jesse, the bodyguard I had before the pairing. That way, when you do need to leave, I won't be alone. Someone will always be here."

Jared chuckled and lifted a brow. "We've not had a reason to have someone here when we were gone."

"Until now," she added.

"Until now," he agreed. "As you said, you have my phone. It's untraceable so if you need me, or any of us, do not hesitate to call."

She nodded. "Have fun and I'll see you soon." She watched her men as they left the kitchen and heard their chatter fade in the distance.

***

Olivia retrieved the last of the cupcakes from the oven and turned it off. She checked the time. It was just after ten in the evening. She sat the icing to the side and rolled out the fondant she'd made earlier. Picking up the fondant knife, she traced on the suits in a deck of cards; two hearts, spade, club, and diamond. Then carved a crown.

Maybe they would enjoy the sentiment. Maybe she could get Landon to paint them in a portrait, the king, his Jacks, and their Queen.

The doorbell chimed. She put the knife down and wiped her hands on a towel, then headed out of the kitchen.

Her heels echoed with each step she took. The house was empty. It felt almost haunted in a way.

She leaned against the door. "Who is it?" she asked and peeked out the hole. A deliveryman stood on the other side, and he held a crate. Excitement spilled over and she squealed. Sherlock was here.

"Delivery. I have a cat in a crate. He needs to be signed for."

She opened the door with a grin. "Ooh, where is my baby?"

The man handed over a tablet and she signed her name. He then picked up the crate and handed it over.

"Thanks, have a great day," the man told her.

"Thank you. You as well." She closed the door and sat the crate down, opening it. Sherlock meowed and padded out onto the marble floor, then to her arms. She picked him up and he rubbed his face on hers.

"Oh, baby boy, I missed you so much!"

A knock sounded on the door. She put Sherlock down and stood. "Did you come with brothers or something?" she teased her cat. He merely meowed up to her. She opened the door, not looking see who may be on the other side.

"Did you forget something?" she started when she opened the door. The man on the other side removed a cover as dark as midnight from his head. She gasped. She did not expect *him* to be on the other side of the door. Dressed in a dark gray suit, tailored to him, blood red tie, and white button-down shirt, stood the evil man from the claiming ceremony. She pushed the door partially closed. "Victor. What are you doing here?"

He tugged the leather gloves from his hands and pushed them into his pockets. "Are your men home? Do they have time for an audience with me?" he asked and leered as he leaned into the doorjamb.

Wasn't that convenient.

He shows up when the men are gone.

Olivia didn't believe in coincidences, but right now she was willing to make an exception for Victor's appearance to their home.

"Well, actually, no. But you can—"

"Then, I'll wait for them," Victor said and pushed past her.

"I didn't invite you in."

"You know that doesn't work on us? That's Hollywood shit. I can come and go as I please."

Anger peaked and she reached out for him, grabbing his arm. She tugged on his arm. "Not in this house you can't. You need to leave. I'll let them know you stopped by."

"Well, actually," he turned to face her and took her hand off his arm. He squeezed it tight and she wanted to scream out. She also did not want to give him the satisfaction of crying out. "I came for you. Bonus for me, you're alone."

"No, you need to leave. Now. I don't want you here alone with me." Fear rose alongside her anger, as well as adrenaline. Was this a fight or flight moment? Could she outrun him if he tried to attack her? "You can either wait outside for them to return, or you can leave. Either way, they will be back soon."

A devious grin tugged the corners of his mouth. "Not if I can help it they won't be."

"What?" she whispered and took a step back. She yanked her hand free and massaged the pain from it that he'd caused. "What do you mean?"

He shrugged with a malevolent chuckle. "They have something I want. And when I want something, I always get it."

She shook her head and Sherlock hissed. Victor spied her cat and sneered. She took advantage of his distraction and sprinted down the hall.

A force hit her from behind, knocking the breath from her lungs. She hit the ground hard and weight bared down on her. Her hair was pulled, forcing her head back. A hiss next to her ear, "Mine," he growled and licked her neck. "Filthy blood whore!" He spit on the floor and yanked her head once more. "They fed on you already?"

She coughed, air rushing back to her lungs. "Fuck you!" she screamed.

"Did you drink from them?"

"Fuck you!"

He growled and pulled her hair, forcing her head to the side, her cheek on the floor. "Answer me!"

"Fuck you!" she screamed again. Sherlock hissed and growled in the background. Maybe her cat would jump on the man attacking her, but if he did, Victor would kill him. She prayed he would stay back.

"What do you want from me?" she cried, her eyes blurred with tears.

Would she live through this evening?

Did he plan on keeping her alive?

Did he set up this shit to trap her?

"You, Olivia. I want you." Then, Victor pressed a rag over her face. Dizziness overcame her and her vision blurred and began to darken.

Shit, was this chloroform?

Panic shot through her veins like ice water. She could not move and her vision darkened until everything turned black.

***

Olivia blinked and groaned. She lifted her head and pain erupted in her neck, causing her head to thump in agony. She hissed and her throat stung like she'd swallowed liquid fire. She tried to move her arms but couldn't. She began to panic, her breathing coming in erratic pants. Waking from zero to adrenaline was not a smart move. Dizziness and nausea plagued her.

She took a deep breath, trying to force herself to calm and to gain an understanding of her surroundings. Lifting her gaze to the ceiling, she noted her arms were bound above her head. She hung like a limp doll. Her wrists burned and fatigue set in. Her arms ached. Her skin was chaffed from the metal. She swallowed the dryness in her throat and lowered her gaze.

She gasped at the dried blood crusted on her body, her arms, her breasts. She still had some clothes on, but not much was left. Further down, her legs were also bound with metal shackles around her ankles. Her legs, like her arms, had slash marks on them.

Shit, where the hell am I?

She inspected her surroundings. She appeared to be in a dungeon of sorts. The walls were cold and felt like cement. A slow drip echoed in the background. The stir of wind was heard, but nothing else. Images of King Arthur's castle came to mind from the storybooks she read.

Did Victor do this?

Victor!

Shit!

She was gone and her men would not know where she was, or how to find her.

Jared's phone!

It was in her pocket before. She pressed her backside to the wall in hopes of feeling the phone in her pocket, but nothing.

No phone.

No fucking phone.

Sherlock.

Was her cat okay?

"Ahh, sleeping beauty lives," came Victor's voice. She heard footsteps and the shadows moved. He stepped into the light with a sadistic grin. His shirt was tainted with blood, probably hers. He had dried blood around his mouth that ran down his neck. Her neck throbbed with ever thump of her heartbeat.

Shit, if he bit me, and drained my blood, he could very well kill me.

Dammit, Jared, my stable, I'm sorry.

Victor rested his foot on something. In the shadows it was hard to tell what it was, but Olivia was positive it was a body. But of who?

As if answering her question, he kicked the form forward. A man rolled a few feet from her, his eyes open, deadpanned. He did not breathe or move. He was dead. Her breathing hitched and she muddled a scream.

"Who was that?" she cried out.

"My messenger boy. He was in on the plan with me to get you here. Well, that is, until you arrived. He then had a change of heart, so I had to kill him."

"You're a monster," she whispered and closed her eyes. She needed water. She needed blood. She needed her stable.

"Did you know I had a contract on you?"

She looked up at him. "What? You couldn't have had a contract on me. You're an idiot. Let me go."

"Sure." He stepped toward her and lifted her chin with his finger. "Be mine and I'll give you your freedom."

She chuffed a laughed. "Right. Be yours by becoming your prisoner. How is that freedom?"

He bent down to her, his nose grazing hers. He rested a palm on the wall next to her head. "Be mine."

He smelled foul. His entire being reeked of the odor of death. "No, fuck you." She swallowed the bile climbing up her throat. "Let me go! My stable will find me and when they do—"

"What?" He chuckled. "Your stable? Kill me? No, I don't think so." Victor placed his hands on her breasts and squeezed them together.

The bile rose and threatened to spew vomit on his chest. "Do not touch me!"

"Oh, but I already did." He leaned in and licked her neck.

Her neck stung from pain before, but with his touch, it erupted in pain. "Did you feed from me without permission?"

"You were knocked out," he whispered. "I couldn't exactly ask you. There was no need to anesthetize you, either."

He bit her like a damn savage. She growled, and using all her strength, she thrust her head forward and head butted him. The pain that erupted was nothing compared to the triumph she felt in giving him what he deserved.

"You bitch!" he yelled out. Victor slapped her face. It stung like hell. He grabbed her by the cheek and forced her face forward. "You will be mine!"

"You are no better than a man who drugs a woman with the intention of raping her!"

He chuckled, patted her cheek, and forced his lips on hers.

She opened her mouth and when his tongue slipped in, she bit it.

Hard.

"Fuck," he growled and pulled away. He spit blood on the floor. Victor raised his hand again.

"It takes a real man to strike a woman who's bound with no way to defend herself. Go you," she spoke.

He snarled and leaned in. He squeezed her cheeks and he opened his mouth to speak when someone cleared their throat. Victor smirked and pulled away. He licked his lips.

She felt sick.

"You said you would keep me. Why do you need her if you have me?"

Olivia recognized the familiar voice, a voice she did not expect to hear. Out of the shadows stepped Candace. Olivia snarled at her. "Are you fucking kidding me right now?"

Candace laughed and crossed her arms over her chest. "Your men were hot and, damn, the fucking I could have received." She shook her head. "I had a choice; them or Victor. Honestly, I wanted Victor. He was a sure thing. I want to serve, not be served. There is a difference, you know?"

"And, there's a difference in being a bitch and being a nasty, overused cunt, no one would ever touch!" Olivia retorted.

Candace screamed and leapt toward her. Victor caught the blood demon mid-jump and thrust her body against the wall. His hand grabbed Candace's throat. "You touch her, I kill you. Understand?"

Olivia watched as the reality of the situation Candace put herself in, choosing this masochist over a new life, dawned on the woman. Or maybe it was the realization of the mistake she had just made. Or it was Candace seeing the error of her ways. Or maybe Candace simply hurt her precious little head.

A tear slipped down Candace's cheek. She nodded and lowered her gaze, submitting. Victor released her and Candace dropped to her knees.

"Leave us," Victor told her. "Now!"

She flinched and met Olivia's gaze. Candace stood and let her gaze drop to the floor, then left the room.

Olivia closed her eyes and redirected her focus to how to alert her men. She recalled what they'd told her about their blood bond. If she were scared, even on the other side of the earth, they would know. Well, right now, she feared her own life and needed them to find her.

Is it like following a beacon?

Would they know to come here?

Please, come find me.

I'm in a dungeon with Victor.

Please.

She opened her eyes and met Victor's gaze. She needed to stall him, if possible. She needed to keep herself alive and buy her stable time to find her. "Tell me about this contract," she asked.

"The contract?" Victor crossed the room to her. "It was with your mother."

Olivia's eyes and mouth widened. To say she was shocked was an understatement.

My mother?

No, not possible.

No way.

"Lies," she yelled.

"Would you like to see it? I was there when your father fucked her and you were created. Every child Lucious made, I have ownership over."

"You watched them? What are you, some kind of voyeur sadist?" She furrowed her brows. "Who the hell is Lucious?"

He smirked. "Let's just say I enjoy watching. As for Lucious? He's your father." Victor leaned into her and ran a finger over her check, down her neck, and circled her nipple.

"For fuck sake, Victor, don't touch me!"

He grinned and cupped her breast with his hand. "When he told me about your mother..." He squeezed it, pinching her nipple once more. "I approached her. I promised her she would be set for life. She eagerly agreed to the contract. However, when you reached of age, her being set for life was unfortunately short lived." Victor smirked.

Olivia shook her head. Her mother sold her unborn child for a life of luxury. Then, before she could actually 'cash in', she died.

"Ahh, so you understand?" he asked.

She met his glare. "You...you killed my mother?"

He smirked and grabbed her cheek again. "My love..." His nose grazed against her cheek. "I simply put the motions into place. Poison can sometimes take a long time to process when it needs to be undetected."

A breath rushed from her lips and bile rose again. This time, she dry heaved. Victor pushed her face away and he stepped back with a manic-filled laugh.

She needed to escape.

She needed her stable.

She needed to fight for her life.

Chapter Thirteen

JARED, JAKE, ETHAN, Landon, and Aidan stood in the council meeting room, waiting for the elders to arrive. The room walls were red with velvet texture, the floors hardwood. Jared regarded the empty mahogany desk and raised his brow. Paintings hung on the wall and figurines stood on the desktop, but no one from the council was in sight. He checked his watch and flashed Jake a side glance.

"What the hell? They never—" Jared buckled over as if he were punched in the gut. He groaned and pressed his hands on his thighs. "Fuck," he whispered. "Liv."

Hearing the groans from his brothers, he closed his eyes and focused on Olivia. Something was wrong. Fear pulsed through him from her blood. She was reaching out for them in a desperate way. She called out for her stable of men.

"Fuck!" he groaned louder.

"What is the meaning of this?" came a voice from across the room.

Jared lifted his gaze up to a man dressed as if he stepped off a photo shoot. Malik, one of the elders, stepped into the room. His raven, shoulder length hair, parted down the middle, moved with the air as he made his way across the room. "What the hell is all this? Did you come here to get sick and pass on some fuckery?"

"Fuckery?" Jake echoed. "Fuck no, something's wrong."

"Did you call us here?" Jared asked.

Malik bent down and lifted Jared's face to meet his own. He shook his head. "No. Neither I, nor anyone here, made any call for you or your men."

"Someone came by," Jared groaned again and shook his head. "Someone told us you called. Shit, we need to go. Something is wrong with our concubine."

"Then go to her," Malik told him and took Jared by his elbow. "Is there any reason your lady would be in peril?"

Jared shook his head. "No. I cannot think..." He paused and met Ethan's gaze. Jared nodded, as if reading his mind. "Victor." He turned back to Malik.

"Are you positive? Allegations can turn fatal, Jared."

Jared nodded. "Yeah, I'm sure. We, shit..." He groaned. "We need to go."

"Then, I'll come along with you and bring my guards. I can see you're in trouble. If Victor is truly causing this, we'll find him and rescue your lady. If it is him, or whoever is causing this, will answer for his or her crimes. They will answer for lying about posing as elders as well."

Jared nodded and attempted to hold off the pain he felt. The others did nothing to hide it. Aidan cried out while Landon pressed his palms on the crimson walls. "I thank you, sir," Jared told him. "And, if it's not too much to ask—"

Malik nodded. "I'll drive. Let's go. Now."

The quintuple rushed through the elder's coven with Malik and two of his guards in tow. The halls of red velvet whisked by in a breeze as the men ran.

Olivia, Jared spoke to her through his mind. He knew she could not hear him, but he spoke to her anyway.

We are on our way.

Hold strong.

Hold true.

We are coming and we'll find where you are and destroy that son-of-a-bitch.

They reached the garage and Jared opened the SUV. He handed his keys to Malik. The men climbed in and Malik started the car. Jared groaned and held onto his stomach.

"What the fuck is happening," Landon asked.

"I can't go through this again," Aidan groaned. "Maxine... My Maxine. I could feel her dying and did not get to her in time. It was like this."

"The fuck that will happen today," Jared growled.

Malik put the SUV into gear, pressed the gas, and the tires squealed as they left the garage.

"Do you know where you're going?" Jake asked from the backseat.

Jared remembered his phone. He had worked with a computer technician to put all their phones on a shared network. All phones were untraceable but could still find one another's. "Ping my phone. She had my cell."

Jake pulled out his phone and pressed the locate button. It lit on the screen, but the phone was at their home. "It's at home. She's not there. I can feel it."

"Mother fucker," Jared whispered and turned to Malik. "Turn down the main street away from the coven. We're running on instinct here." He laid his head back and addressed his brother. "Jake, if you feel a pull, you have to speak up!"

"*Madre del fottuto,*" Landon groaned.

"You said, mother of the fucking?" Ethan asked.

Jared growled. "Stop fucking around. Where is Olivia?"

Ethan rested his forehead on the seat in front of him. "Aidan, who was it that came to the door?"

"Dude, I said I didn't know," Aidan told him.

"I'm not questioning you, I'm curious if they have something to do with this," Ethan said.

"What did he look like?" Malik asked. "Did he give a name?"

"He was a dark haired young man. He said he was a messenger for the elders and I think he said his name was Brian?" Aidan offered.

"You didn't mention a name before," Jared said.

"I didn't think to mention it before," Aidan told him.

"There is no Brian with the coven," Malik said when he turned down a street.

Jared shook his head. "Maybe to stage a distraction?"

"Yeah. Who would want to get Olivia from us? Who has an end goal to get something they want?" Jake asked.

Jared growled. "Victor". When he said his name, the entire car erupted in an uproar of shared rage. It was time for revenge.

***

Olivia pulled at her restraints. Pain shot through her body and blood trickled down her arms. Across the room, she watched as Candace paced the floor. Occasionally, the blood demon would make eye contact. When she did, Candace would snarl. Victor's phone rang and when he pulled it from his pocket, he stepped out of the room.

Olivia needed to do something. Candace may be her only option. Taking a chance, she spoke to her. "Why are you doing this?"

"How dare you speak to me!" Candace yelled. She crossed the room to her and grabbed Olivia's throat and squeezed. Her nails dug into her skin. "Do you realize you ruined everything for me?"

"Let me go," Olivia snarled. "Let me go right now!"

Candace pushed her away, then slapped her. "Fuck you!"

"No, fuck you," Olivia yelled back. "I did nothing to you. You showed up at my house to feed and get fed on."

"Because you couldn't do it!" she said. "I could have had them for myself, all of them. But, no..." Candace eyed Olivia from top to bottom, then sneered. "You had to grow fucking balls and take them from me."

"They were never yours to begin with!" Olivia pulled on her arms and exacerbated the dread that pulled at her nerves. Her wrists and ankles burned. Her shoulders ached. "But, this here?" Olivia shook the restraints and growled. "This is all you, Candace! All you! If you stop this now, I'll tell the elders you had nothing to do with this, and you were also held as a prisoner."

"What?" The woman laughed. "Why would you do that? That is the most ridiculous thing I've ever heard!"

"Are you not a prisoner? Has he fed you? Have you fed from him? No, I don't think you have. Look at me! He has mutilated my body! For what?" She gritted her teeth through the pain in her arms. "If you let me go, I'll go with you to the elders. We'll make our case known, that Victor acted alone."

The crazy, hate-all-women stare Candace was giving began to fade.

Realization in Olivia's words appeared to be ringing true. A tear slipped down Candace's cheek and she quickly swiped it away. "Why would you help me?"

"Because I understand what this means to you. Until I fed from them, I did not understand the bond, the need, what feeding does to the blood demon. After I experienced it for myself, I was able to understand. Candace, you deserve a second chance." Whether Olivia necessarily believed that or not, right now, she would say anything to get this woman to help her. She truly could understand the addiction to the blood. She had only one taste of her men and knew there was no going back.

Candace dropped to her knees and cried into her hands. "What have I done?" she whispered.

"Candace, quick, release me before he comes back!" When she did not move, Olivia yelled her name. "Candace!"

Candace lifted her gaze and met Olivia's. She nodded and quickly got to her feet. She crossed the room and fidgeted with the shackles on Olivia's arms.

"It's no use. I don't have the key," Candace whispered.

"What the *fuck* do you think you're doing?" Victor growled.

Both women gasped and looked at Victor as he stepped into the room. He reached behind his back and pulled out a gun. From the distance, it appeared to be a nine-millimeter weapon. He cocked the chamber and pointed it toward the women.

"Get the fuck away from her, Candace. Now, before I kill you!"

Candace cried out and pointed to Olivia. "She made me do it!" She crawled on the floor toward Victor and grabbed his ankle. "Please, don't punish me. She did it. It's her fault!"

Olivia rolled her eyes. "Sure, whatever. All my fault. Victor, you won't get away with this. My stable will be here. They will find me. And, if you're lucky, you'll receive a quick death."

Victor grinned. "I like a strong, confident woman." He kicked Candace off his foot. "But, you're mistaken, my love."

"I am *not* your love. Do not ever call me that again." She yanked again at her restraints.

"Leave it be," Victor told her. He reached for Candace and grabbed a handful of her hair, pulling her to her feet. Candace screamed out and Victor pushed her out in front of him. He held the gun to her head. "Stop trying to break free!"

Olivia stopped fidgeting and stared, mouth agape, at Candace. The woman sobbed and reached for Victor's hands. "Stop it," Candace cried out. "Stop!" She held Olivia's gaze and tears made her eyes look black, like raccoons.

Fear clenched at Olivia's heart. A gun to her head and all Candace wanted was a fix. An addict given syringes filled with her drug of choice, but every time she reached for it, the syringe moved that much further away. Like a donkey chasing a dangling carrot.

Victor raised the gun above Candace's head and brought it down hard. She fell to the floor, knocked out.

Olivia stared at her body, wide eyed. "Oh my God, did you kill her?"

"No," he said and tucked the gun away. He reached into his pocket and pulled out a switch knife. He pressed a button and it opened with a click. "She'll live."

"What... Don't come near me with that," she said and shook her head. Her heart sped up and her breathing became erratic.

Victor stood in front of her and brought the knife to her face. Olivia could see her own reflection in the steel. He moved it down over her breast, resting the sharp blade on her delicate skin. "I could slice you open, drain all your blood, and leave you for death. Or, you could accept my offer and be mine."

She snarled and bit the inside of her cheek. Iron pooled in her mouth and she spit on Victor's face. "I would rather die!"

He grinned. "I love your spirit, but your stable," he whispered and raised the knife to her inner arm. He sliced through her skin like a hot knife on butter. She screamed and blood seeped down her arm. "What would they do without their precious concubine?" He brought the blade to her cheek and sliced her open, temple to lip.

Olivia cried out and her body shook. She was losing too much blood. Her body convulsed and the last image she saw was Victor smirking before her vision blurred to darkness.

***

"Wake up and face me."

A faint voice, muffled slightly, called to Olivia. She blinked her eyes open and found herself in a dark room...or maybe she was outside. It was hard to tell.

"Olivia," whispered the voice. "Come on, wake up, lover. I'm not done with you."

Olivia shifted but could not move. Her arms were held above her head. She struggled and the events with Victor flooded back. Fear escalated and she panted for breath.

Liv, we're coming, my love.

Hold on a little longer.

A faint voice whispered in her mind and she gasped. "Jared? Is that you?" A soft light in the distance interrupted the darkness. She could make out a man's figure. It appeared to be the outline of Jared, but was it him? Where were the others?

"Can you see me? Help me! I need you!" she cried.

Pain shot through her legs. She groaned and looked down. The softness of the light illuminated her body just enough, she could see blood oozing from her thighs. Her eyes widened.

"There she is," Victor said.

Olivia lifted her head up and met Victor's gaze. She cried out, "Please, let me go or kill me."

The light disappeared and her fear spiraled. A hand grabbed her arm and she gasped. Seeking who took hold of her, she found Jared. Relief flooded her as he stood next to her. She reached for him just as his grip lifted. She reached for him again and the restraints held her back. Jared had moved away, distance between them. She tried to reach once more, but the more she tried the farther away he appeared to be. She felt like Alice falling down the rabbit hole.

"Wake up, dammit!" Victor slapped her face and Olivia opened her eyes.

She cried, slumping into her body weight. "Kill me, please!" she begged. Her head lolled down. She was too weak to hold it up any longer. She blinked slowly as blood oozed into her vision. Her body was red with crimson. Soon, she would bleed out and she would finally die.

Soon, this would be over.

Soon...

***

Then, a crash erupted the silence. Victor growled and released Olivia. Her eyes closed, most likely passed out again. He wiped his knife on his pants, then closed it and tucked it into his pocket. He marched out of the dungeon and closed the wooden door, locking it.

The hall that led to the dungeon was dark and smelled like death. The corridor was dark, spider webbed like something from a horror scene. Torches lit the hall as he made his way to the exit. He opened the door and was met with a punch to the face.

Victor fell back and held his nose and yelled out. "Damn you! This is my home!"

"Not when you may have someone's concubine being held against her will," Malik announced. He stepped inside and massaged his hand.

"You punched me?" Victor asked and looked up at the man entering his home. Flanking him were Olivia's five men. "Get the fuck out of my home!"

"I punched you, yes," Malik answered him. "Olivia's bond with her men is strong enough to lead us here. Why is that?" Malik asked and bent over Victor's body. "I have reason enough to be here, so, no, I will not leave. And, if I find her here, death will become you tonight."

Victor remained silent and pushed away from Malik. He got to his feet and pinched the bridge of his nose. It throbbed and he swiped at his nose, his hand coming away covered in blood.

Victor regarded Olivia's stable, as she called them. Jared, flanked by Jake and Ethan, then Landon and Aidan.

Jared snarled. "Where the *fuck* is she?"

"Suck my dick," Victor yelled. "She's mine!"

Malik sped across the room and pinned Victor to the wall, hand around his throat. "So, you admit she is here?"

"She is mine! I put a contract out on her!"

Malik laughed. "A contract? Are you mad? We do not recognize contracts! It is worthless and will not be recognized in the coven."

"What the fuck is it the coven does, then?" Victor accused.

"The coven writes up agreements where both parties are satisfied. We do not, and never will, take prisoners."

"Can I kill him now?" Jake asked.

"Not yet," Malik said. "Let's find your lady first."

"In here," came a mouse-like voice. Candace peeked out and pointed toward the dungeon hall. Blood had dried across her neck and she brought a hand to her head. "He knocked me out before I could help her."

Jared was on her before she had a chance to react. "Lies! You did this!" He picked her up and pushed her against the wall. "You did this!"

"No, I was trying to help, please," Candace begged.

Victor smirked at the turn of events playing out. Tell me, Aidan. Do you miss your Maxine?"

Jake and Ethan pulled at Jared's arms, forcing him to release Candace, then stopped and turned when Victor spoke. Aidan turned to face him and lifted his brow. "What the fuck did you just say?"

"Yes, your lady was a good fuck before I killed her," Victor announced.

"Fuck," Landon growled. "I have this. Go get our Liv."

"Oh, you're dead, man, you're so fucking dead," Aidan told him. He sped on the man and pushed Malik out of the way. He snarled and pulled his fist back, just as Malik caught it.

"No," the elder told him. "Not like this. Let him go. I will be swift in passing judgment on him. Trust me in this."

Landon pulled on Aidan. "*Lascialo andare, adesso!*"

"No," Aidan snarled. "I will not let him go! He will die for killing my Maxine and for taking our Olivia!"

"Yes, he will," Malik told him. "But not by your hand. Now, let him go before I have my guards remove you."

Aidan released him and fell back in step with Landon. "He's not leaving my fucking sight!"

"*Calmati, fratello*," Landon told him.

Aidan nodded. "I'm cool. You can let me go. I'm good."

Victor turned and watched Jared, Jake, and Ethan speed down the hall.

"Clear!" Jake called.

"Clear," said Ethan.

Jared opened another door and stepped in. "Liv? Olivia? Answer me, I know I'm close!"

***

Olivia was falling down an endless well. She grasped for the walls and tumbled over and over. She felt herself reaching for something, anything to hold onto...until one finally made real estate.

"Liv! Where are you?"

"Jared?" she whispered and lifted her head. Her eyes barely opened and her body shook. She sucked in a deep breath and cried out. "Jared!"

He rushed the room. "In here!"

Jared had found her. Relief filled her and she prayed it was not another tormenting dream. His hands touched her shackles and in that moment, she knew he was real.

"I'm sorry," she whispered. "I'm so sorry."

Two more bodies entered the room and soon, Jake and Ethan joined Jared.

"Why are you sorry," Jared asked her, then paused. The three others stopped moving and in unison, growls filled the emptiness of the room.

"He dies. Tonight." Jared reached for the shackles on her right wrist and pulled. It broke with a loud clang.

She screamed out from the pain that radiated between the shackle and her arm falling to her side. Ethan broke the left shackle and Jake worked on her legs. Her body slumped over and Jared caught her, scooping her up into his arms.

"My love, my Liv. You're alive," Jared whispered and pressed his lips to her forehead.

"I need...blood," she whispered.

Jake pulled his sleeve back and bit into his arm. He pressed it to her lips. She greedily accepted his gift and groaned. His blood pooled in her mouth as she swallowed, drinking him as fast as she could.

"Here, let me," Ethan said and pulled his sleeve up. He bit into his arm and offered his gift to her as well.

She released Jake and took Ethan's arm and drank from him. Her body was slowly beginning to heal. She swallowed one last time and pulled her mouth away. Her arms were still too weak to move. Resting her head against Jared's shoulder, she whispered, "Please, take me home."

Jared carried her into the corridor, followed by Jake and Ethan. She could hear shuffles and screams coming from the end of the hall.

"What's going on?" she asked.

"I think Aidan may be killing Victor," Jake told her.

They stepped out of the hall into the main room where the others had gathered. Olivia recognized Malik, one of the elders. He was with two guards, who both held Victor.

Aidan was like a rabid dog, fighting to get at Victor. He was being held back by Ethan.

"Her blood tasted so sweet on my tongue, even sweeter when she realized she would die," Victor announced.

"I'll kill you," screamed Aidan. "You raped and killed her! You son-of-a-bitch!"

Olivia gasped and her eyes widened. "He did what?"

She felt a growl vibrate from Jared. "Did he rape you?"

"No. Fuck, no," she said. "He hurt me, but he didn't break me."

She felt him sigh with relief. "Victor dies tonight," Jared announced.

"I'd love to kill him," she whispered. "But this kill belongs to Aidan."

"Victor," Malik announced and opened his suit jacket. He pulled out a long silver blade. "You have been found guilty of your crimes. You have been charged with the rape and murder of Maxine, concubine to Aidan. You have been charged with the kidnapping and attempted murder of Olivia, concubine to Jared and his household."

"What about me?"

The group turned to the small voice who had been ignored during this ordeal.

Candace.

"As for you," Malik turned to face her. "If I find you had any part in this, you will be dealt with accordingly."

"Let her go," Olivia told him. "She was a prisoner here, just as I was."

Jared lifted his brow. "Do not lie to the elders," he whispered.

"I'm not," she told him. "She may not have started off as a prisoner, but in the end, she was held against her will. She deserves to be heard."

Malik nodded and approached Candace. "What was your role in this? And tell me the truth as this will be your only chance."

Victor struggled in the grasp of the guards. He growled but would not escape.

Candace sobbed into her hands. "Victor promised to claim me as his pairing. He promised he would feed me, and I from him. He promised..." she trailed off as her sobs grew louder.

"Then you have confessed guilty as an accessory," Malik announced and turned from her.

"Please," Olivia begged.

"Don't," Jared interrupted. "Let the elders do what they need. Stay out of it."

She stared at Jared for a moment, then frowned. "She's an addict. She went off instinct. I can empathize. Since having you, if you were stripped from me, I would lose my mind."

He let out a long sigh, then nodded. "I understand," he whispered.

"I would have fucked Olivia and drained her of her blood! She would have been mine or she would die. You fucking blood whore," he yelled out. "You fed on them, you filthy demon!"

Malik stepped back to Victor and in a move so quick it almost went unseen, he gripped the man's throat. "You have been found guilty."

Victor struggled under his grip and the guards held him in place. Malik leaned in. "Go to hell, you bastard." Malik ripped out Victor's throat, then whipped his silver blade across his neck, slicing through bone and muscle in an instant. Victor's head slid off and bounced on the ground. His body fell in a heap, his stump bleeding out. "Death. Beautiful, gruesome, glorious death."

Malik bent down and wiped off his blade on Victor's dead body, then tucked it into his pocket. "Now, Candace..." He stood and turned to face her. "You will come with me, until we figure out what to do with you."

Candace screamed. "Please, don't kill me!"

"Get her to the car," Malik told his guards. They nodded and took her by the arms, leading her out. He turned to

Jared and touched Olivia on her head. "My child, please, know you are now safe. Victor is no more."

He then turned to Aidan and rested his hands on the man's shoulders. "I wish there was more we could do with what happened to Maxine. The information regarding her death will be updated. Come to the coven when you're ready. We'll discuss her assets."

Aidan nodded and lowered his head. Malik released him and walked out the door, Victor's body and head in tow.

Landon placed a hand on Aiden's shoulder and gave it a squeeze. "It's over, *mio fratello.*"

Olivia sagged in Jared's arms and her eyes burned with tears. This nightmare was over. Her men had found her. She laid her head against Jared's chest. "Please, take me home."

Chapter Fourteen

IT HAS BEEN said, the moment before you die, important memories of your life will flash before your eyes. For Olivia, her life began when she met her stable. A soft, faint, beep repeated over and over. Her body was cold and as much as she tried, she could not force her eyes to open.

Olivia...

She gasped, hearing Jared's voice.

I can't see you.

In the darkness, a light appeared. It was soft and grew in size. Soon, the shape formed into five bodies walking toward her. The bodies faintly corporeal, each of her men came into view. They were smiling, waving, holding their hands out for her. As she reached for them, her hand would pass through theirs.

Jake, her lover of food and experimenting with new things. "Liv, you're my life now. Please, come back."

I'm here...

Landon, her lover of art and creation. "*Bella donna, ti amo.*"

Ethan, her lover who defends those who cannot defend themselves. He approached her and pressed his lips upon her forehead. And she felt him. She reached for him, but her hands passed through his body.

Am I dreaming?

Aidan, her lover of all things beautiful in life. He winked at her. "Wake up, baby girl."

And Jared, her lover who invests in the possibilities of life, and leader of her stable. He closed the distance to her and lifted his hands to cup her face. He tilted her head up and pressed his lips to hers.

A shock hit her body and with a deep breath, Olivia opened her eyes.

She heard the familiar sound of a heart monitor, and a soft murmur of voices.

"She'll make a full recovery. She'll be weak, and she's bruised, but she'll live to fight another day."

Olivia blinked and focused her blurry gaze. The room was lit, but only faintly. A few candles burned in the room. Glancing at the ceiling, then the walls, she realized she was in her room.

In the distance stood a man in a white jacket. She focused her sight on him and as her vision cleared, she realized he was a doctor. He wrote on a clipboard and in front of him, stood Jared.

Meeting her gaze, Jared's brows rose and his eyes widened. "She's awake."

The doctor turned and he smiled. "Hello, Miss Martin. My name is Doctor Kenneth Crane. You've been through quite an ordeal. How are you feeling?"

The doctor appeared to be in his fifties, salt and pepper hair, laugh lines around his eyes and mouth. Was he a human working for the coven?

"Sore," she whispered. "My throat hurts."

"I'm sure it does. There's trauma around your neck from strangulation, but the bruising is healing nicely, as well as the rest of your body. The cuts will leave faint scars."

Her body began to ache as if the word 'cuts' turned on the pain sensors. She closed her eyes and sighed. "What happened to Candace?"

"We'll talk about her later," Jared answered.

She opened her eyes and found him on the other side of her bed. He brushed her hair back from her face, then leaned down and feathered his lips over her forehead. "I thought we were going to lose you," he whispered.

She reached for him, resting her hand on the back of his head. He was real. He was here. Relief settled her beating heart. "It'll take a lot more than a man with a switchblade to get me down."

Jared chuckled. "That's my girl."

"Shall I alert the others she's awake?" Doctor Crane asked.

"Yes, please," Jared answered. "And, thank you for being here today."

"My services are to the coven and their mates." The doctor bowed his head and left the room.

Olivia watched the man leave, then closed her eyes. One question was answered, the doctor worked for the coven. "Is he human?"

"Yes," Jared answered.

"Is he the mate to someone?"

"Like a concubine?" he asked.

She nodded and opened her eyes. "Is he paired?"

"Yes, but he's not a blood demon."

"How does that work, then?" she asked. "I thought humans could not sustain vampires?"

"I don't think that was said. Demon blood is our preferred source; however, humans can sustain us as well. It's dangerous, though. There's the chance of our blood getting into their bodies. If that were to happen, the change would be inevitable."

If Olivia were to bring her friend, Tawne, into this world, there's a chance she could be paired, and survive. She wouldn't be alone in this new world.

But, would Tawne want this?

Would she be okay to go along with the notion of being fed on, day in and day out?

What would happen if she were to become a vampire?

"What's on your mind? Your mood shifted," Jared asked.

She shook her head. "It's nothing. But, Jared?" She took his hand and brought it to her lips. "I left a life behind to be here. You brought me Sherlock, and I appreciate that, but if I'm not able to leave the confines of our home, I need another type of freedom. I need my friends."

"You're not being able to leave is for your own safety, as well as ours. You can still venture into the yards during the daytime and soak up the sun. I need you to do this. I can then smell the sunshine on your skin and imagine taking you on a beach."

She nodded. "I'll do that for you. For all of you." Olivia pictured Tawne on the arm of a vampire...or vampires.

I think all of this would turn her world upside down, but first, I would need to talk to her.

"What is the likeliness I can have my cell phone?"

"I didn't realize you wanted one. Since your life was here... I just assumed... Forgive me," he said with a smile. "I'll have one picked up for you."

"Thank you. Everything has happened so quickly, it wasn't something I really thought I'd want, or need, until now."

"Is there someone you wish to get in touch with?"

She nodded and hope filled her. "Yes. I would love to see my friend, Tawne. She's been through a lot with me. I'd love to bring her here for a visit."

"How would you explain all of this to her?"

"I would have to remind her to be open-minded. She actually has a fascination with darkness and loves vampire stories and movies. I think she'd be excited about this."

Jared chuckled. "So longas you trust her with what you know, then I trust your judgment."

"Who are we judging?"

They turned to the room entrance. Ethan, Jake, Landon, and Aidan stepped inside the room. Her vampires surrounded her bed. Each of her men, their expressions of love and serenity evident upon their features.

Her heart swelled with love and pride. "I need to get something off my chest."

"Your clothes?" Aidan asked with a chuckle.

She grinned and shook her head. "No, not quite."

"Nice, Casanova," Landon said.

How do I say this?

"Growing up, I did not have a close relationship with my mother, and, as you know, I didn't know my father. With everything I knew, learned, and understood about relationships, I thought there was one person for everyone. One man, one woman. The traditional relationship, be as it may. However, my eyes have been opened to the possibility of something more. I have never been in love or allowed anyone to love me. I never knew what it would feel like and always distanced myself. As a blood demon, it would be pointless to love, marry, or have children. I knew what my destiny was. And most of my life, I was depressed. I didn't realize that until I met each of you. Since coming into your lives, since the pairing, since our first feeding, something opened inside of me, something new. I feel like my heart is on my sleeve, totally exposed, and each of you have a place in it. And, honestly, it scares the hell out of me. I never thought loving more than one person was a possibility, but I love each of you. I am in love with each of you. I don't want to be just your concubine. I want to be your life mate. I want to be yours, because each of you," she paused and felt her eyes burn with the treat of tears. "You're mine." She sat up in her bed and held her arms open. Jared sat on her left, Jake on her right. Landon and Ethan sat behind them, and Aidan held the foot of her bed. She grasped Jared and Jake's hands, and Ethan, Landon, and Aidan placed their hands on her legs. "You are all mine."

"Ours," Jared told her.

"Ours," the others repeated.

Pride swelled inside her and she smiled with a soft laugh.

"I'm happy to see everyone here," Doctor Crane announced when he stepped back into the room. "I have some news."

"Well, let's hear it, Doc," Aidan said.

He closed Olivia's file and held it under his arm. "All your tests are conclusive in healing. You'll be fine to live your life normally," he paused with a smile. "Starting tomorrow."

She sighed with relief and laid back down in her bed. "This is the best news I've heard in a long while."

"Thank you, doctor," Jared said. "Your help has been astronomical."

Doctor Crane nodded. "You're very welcome. I'll be on my way. I'll have my staff come and collect the equipment tonight." And with that, the doctor left the room.

"There's more good news," Ethan offered.

"Oh?" Olivia asked.

"Very good news," Jake added. "The elders claimed Victor's homestead. They were able to sell the estate to another vampire stable."

"Okay," Olivia said and furrowed her brows. "Why is this good news?"

Landon took her hand in his. "The money they acquired will go to concubines who have lost their vampires, for rehabilitation."

"What?" she whispered. Her thoughts went to Candace.

"Yes," Aidan said. "If a concubine loses her vampire for whatever reason, they will now have choices, not just put into volunteer rotation."

She looked at Jared, then.

He nodded. "Consider Malik moved by your actions to help Candace rather than wanting her punished. It's because of you the coven is doing this. No one else has stood up for another concubine like you did."

She squeezed Landon's hand and reached for Jared's with her other. "A part of me felt for her. I understood the pain. If I lost any of you, hell, all of you, I don't know what I would do. I could easily see myself fall down the rabbit hole Candace found herself in. I would do anything, say anything, to have the sensation of feeding, and being fed, one more time."

"Candace has been moved," Jake told her. "She was relocated to another coven across the states. There was a need and she will be used to fulfill purpose."

"Is said purpose for a pairing?" she asked.

"As far as I know, yes, but I'm not certain. One coven does not answer to another," Jake answered. "Think of us as our own governments."

"There's still so much for me to learn about this world," Olivia said with a sigh.

"But, until then, I'm happy here, by myself with each of you."

"Let's give her some rest," Jared told the group as he stood from her bed. "She'll need her energy soon." He bent down and pressed his lips to hers. "Rest well. We'll come for you tomorrow night."

She nodded and touched his face, then turned on her side. One by one, her men filed out of her room. A smile crested her lips. She closed her eyes, allowing sleep to consume her.

***

Olivia's chest rose and fell in fast pulses. She struggled to make it to the end of the hall, but it was as if the ground was molasses and she sunk further into the ground the harder she tried to run. She reached for the wall and pressed her palm against the dark wood grain. Olivia looked behind her and closing the distance was Victor. He wielded a dagger and he bared his fangs. It appeared as if he were flying through the air.

"No!" She sat up with a start, panting for air. She was in her room, in her bed. She closed her eyes and laid back down, thankful for her reality, not the demented one mind-fucking her.

"You may experience symptoms of PTSD," Doctor Crane had warned her. The conversation came back to her as she swiped the sweat from her brow.

A knock at the door sounded. She sat up and pulled the sheet up over her chest. Her men saw every inch of her body, but they'd listened to her and brought Jesse onto their payroll, and into their home. She didn't want Jesse walking in on her birthday suit.

"Liv?" It was Jake.

She sighed. "Come in, I'm okay." The door opened and he peeked inside.

"Are you all right?" he asked.

She nodded. "It was a dream. She motioned for him to come in. "I dreamed I was back at Victor's. He was chasing me with a knife."

Jake sat down on her bed and took her hand in his. "He can no longer hurt you."

She nodded. "I know. PTSD, I suppose."

"In time, it'll pass." He scooted closer to her and Olivia leaned into his body. His arms encircled her, securing her in an embrace. "Other than the dream, how are you feeling?"

"Actually, I feel amazing. Look." She pulled the cover down and exposed her breasts and stomach to him.

Jake growled and Olivia met his gaze. It was the sexiest thing, like the most seductive music calling to her. "I am looking, and damn, woman."

She grinned. "That's not what I want to show you, but I'm glad I still have an effect on you."

He reached for her breast and leaned in. He tilted his lips across hers. "You will forever have an effect on me."

She laughed softly and pulled back. "Okay, seriously, look at my arm." She held her left arm up in the air. "The fucker cut me from elbow to arm pit. There's barely a scar!"

He ran a tentative finger over her healing wound. "I can see that. This is incredible." He reached for her face and tilted her head back. "The scars on your cheek and neck have faded to almost nothing."

Olivia closed her eyes and sighed. Her worst fear was being cut into a grotesque appearance. "I'm so glad," she whispered.

"She's awake!" Aidan called from the hall. "May I come in?"

She looked up at him and nodded. "Of course, but before we start the let's-examine-Liv-for-scars-and-touch-her-body doctor session, I need to shower and clean up." She lifted her brow and grinned. A shower with her stable would be perfect.

"Oh hell, that look," Jake groaned. "She's planning something."

"Evil, that's some evil shit there," Aidan teased.

She laughed and shook her head. "Okay, leave, please. Let me get cleaned up. When I'm ready for you, you'll know to come find me."

Both men stood with Cheshire grins. "Hot damn," Jake said and he backed out of the room.

"What's going on?" Landon appeared in the hall, trailed by Ethan and Jared.

"She's planning something naughty, I think," Aidan said and rubbed his hands together. "Look at her. Pure evil!"

Olivia laughed and stepped from her bed, naked, before her vampires. She wondered if they might drool. She grinned, imagining them wiping their faces, then remembered Jared when he first went down on her. The way his face glistened with her orgasm. Her knees weakened.

In unison, each of them groaned. Jared leaned on the wall. Jake and Landon rubbed their crotches. She knew exactly what she was doing to them. She winked and made her way to her bathroom. "Remember, I'll..." she paused and lifted her brow again. "Summon you."

"Oh hell," Jared muttered and shook his head. "She's definitely feeling better."

As she closed the door, Olivia laughed once more and locked the handle. She didn't trust them to not come into the shower with her, but, damn, that would be hot.

Olivia turned on the water, brushed her teeth, then tested the heat under the shower head. Perfect. She stepped inside and the heat relaxed her. Any remnants of her dream went down the drain.

She was bruised, she was beaten, but she was not broken. Victor, or anyone, would never take that from her. With the protection of her stable, no one could ever get to her again, or would not dare try.

After she washed her hair and body, she imagined what she would wear for her men. Wrapping a towel around her damp hair, she towel-dried her body and padded across her room to her closet. She scanned her clothes but nothing looked promising, which was saying something. Her closet was stocked with clothes.

She decided on option two: her robe. She grabbed a pair of black stilettos: the platform sides resembled the lace up of a corset and the back heel was silver, patterned with snakeskin. She made her way back to the bathroom and removed the towel from her head, then hung it up next to her robe. She tugged the silk robe around her body, the chill of the fabric giving her a slight shiver. She stood in front of her vanity and sat in the powder chair. She considered the stilettos for a moment and decided they needed a pairing of thigh-highs.

She went back into her bedroom and opened her dresser. From inside, she pulled out a pair of thigh-highs that were laced up the back with ribbon. She grinned and slipped them on over her legs. Walking back to her bathroom, she picked up her stilettos and pulled them on. She lifted a brow and smiled at her reflection.

Definitely doable, but something was missing. Gloves. She needed gloves. Pulling open one of the drawers of her vanity, she spied a few pairs of ballroom gloves and grinned. She snagged a black, elbow-length pair.

She sat them on the vanity and took a seat. After applying some eye shadow and liner, she powered her face then applied dark red lipstick. Picking up her blow dryer, she dried her hair, then set it in a bun on the crown of her head. She pulled on her raven-colored silk gloves and smoothed her hands over them. She picked up a pair of diamond earrings, a pearl bracelet, and pearl necklace, putting them on her body. The look reminded her of *Audrey Hepburn* from *Breakfast at Tiffany's*.

She stood and turned left, then right, checking out the final package in the mirror. She nodded to herself and tightened her robe around her body. She thought of one more addition. She pulled a black sash from her vanity and tucked it into her robe pocket.

Opening her bedroom door, Olivia peeked out and did not see anyone waiting for her. She smirked and closed the door behind her. Each step of her heels echoed down the hall. She took the steps down, her gloved hand holding onto the handrail. At the bottom was the fountain room. It was empty.

Good.

They'll find me soon.

Olivia made her way to the game room. Inside, sat a pool and foosball table, beanbag chairs, a bar, fully stocked, and a large flat screen TV. In the corner of the room hung a sex swing. She walked over toward it with a grin.

I'm glad we had this installed with the option to take it down.

Imagine visitors coming over, seeing it.

She picked up the TV remote from one of the shelves in the room and turned it on. She changed it to a rock music station. She sat the remote down and grasped one of the straps to the swing in her hand. She ran her thumb over the material.

Olivia pulled out the black sash from her pocket, then disrobed and laid it across the bar. The cold air gave her chills across her body and her nipples became taut. She fidgeted with her ponytail, then walked to the center of the room. She knelt down and blindfolded herself. She laid her hands down in her lap, bowed her head, and closed her eyes.

Come to me, she called.

Find me.

Feed from me.

Fuck me.

Olivia repeated this only once before she heard what sounded like a stampede in the hall. She pressed her lips together to keep from giggling. Then, the door opened.

Excitement rushed through her body and she had to fight to keep from smiling. She heard the door close and two of her men groan. Landon and Ethan?

"Oh, you are a very, very naughty woman," whispered Jake.

"Damn, baby girl," Aidan groaned.

"Gods, she is beautiful," Ethan spoke.

"*Una dea, bella donna*," Landon whispered.

She heard him say *bella donna* enough times to understand beautiful woman.

Where was Jared?

Why had no one touched her?

Insecurity taunted her mind and she considered removing the blindfold. Just as she fidgeted her fingers, a hand grasped her hair and tugged her head back.

She gasped and hands cradled her head. Lips captured hers and a tongue swiped against hers. She recognized his taste, his passion, his heat.

Jared.

He tightened his grip and pulled her head back once more. "Mine," he growled.

"Yours," she whispered. "I am yours. All of you, I am yours."

Jared tilted her head to the side and she felt him sit down behind her. His chest was naked against her back and she leaned into him. He licked her neck then slicked into her flesh. She inhaled a sharp breath and moaned an exhale. Body heat rose inside her and as if a switch were flipped, her body came alive.

Her arms were extended outward. Two licks, one on each forearm. Two sets of fangs sinking into her flesh.

"*Bella donna*," Landon whispered and cupped her breasts, then squeezed them together. He licked her left nipple, then the right. His tongue circled around her pebbled flesh and he sucked it into his mouth, grazing it with his teeth. He released the swollen nub, moving over to the other and repeating the process, but this time his fangs pierced her flesh.

Olivia bucked to the sensations escalating throughout her body. Someone fondled her other breast. Aidan, maybe? His tongue slicked around her nipple and he bit down. Five sets of hands held her, and each mouth pulled her gift, her blood, her life force.

"Oh my God," she whispered.

Jared pulled away from her neck and his tongue slicked over her wound. His lips feathered over her ear and he whispered, "Exquisite." She felt him move his hand from her shoulder down to her waist and around her body. His finger slipped between her labia, plunging into her heat. "Brothers, she's so fucking wet right now."

A rushed breath left her lips. "Don't stop, please." Her arms were released and lowered. Her breasts were also licked once more and let go.

"Lay with me," Jared whispered. He placed his hands underneath her arms and lifted her upon his body. He laid back and Olivia rested her backside onto his front. "Lift your legs, lover."

She did as he asked.

"Can we take a moment to appreciate the package tonight, brothers?" Ethan announced. "Sexy shoes, the hose with the lace, the gloves, and her blindfold. How the fuck did we get so lucky?"

The others groaned in agreement, and Olivia's lifted the corners of her lips into a smile.

"Lube her," Jared ordered.

A moment later, warm lube dribbled between her ass cheeks and someone pushed a thick finger into her puckered hole.

A soft moan left her lips.

"She's so fucking wet," Jake announced.

She felt Jared move his arm. His cock touched her ass and she sat up.

"Let me help." Olivia climbed off his body and held her arms out. "I need someone to—"

Someone took her hands. "I have you, *mio amore.*"

Landon took a firm grip on her and steadied Olivia as she lowered herself back down over him until the head of his cock pushed into her rear entrance.

"Easy, baby," Jared whispered.

"I'm okay," she told him and her channel surrounded him completely.

"Lay back on me, lover," Jared told her and pressed his palms to her back.

Olivia laid back and he moved his hands to her hips. Lifting her slightly, he pulled out and pushed back into her.

"Oh, yes," she groaned. "Yes, harder. Please, more."

Jared groaned and thrust his cock into her hole, his body slapping against her ass.

"Honey is pouring from her cunt," Landon announced, his voice dark, gravely. "*Voglio scoparti.*"

Olivia's lips parted and she whimpered. "Landon, what did you say?"

A finger pressed against her clit and she screamed. An orgasm on the brink of explosion had erupted.

"I want to fuck you," Landon growled. "I want to see you squirt, *mio amore.*" He moved his finger back and forth in a speed so fast her legs and hips bucked. "Hold her legs," he ordered.

Two of her men took her legs and pulled them toward her chest. Landon pushed his finger inside her and curled it against her sensitive spot. "Come on my hand, *mio amore.*"

"No, I want you to fuck me," Olivia whimpered.

She heard a growl and someone chuckle.

Hands pressed against the inside of her thighs, spreading her legs further apart. Then a tongue, a magnificent lashing of tongue, licked and consumed her throbbing clit.

"Holy shit," she screamed. "Oh my God!" Her body bucked again and the hands on her body pressed her down harder. His lips sucked her clit into his mouth and he growled into her pussy.

It was Landon.

Holy fuck, Landon.

Her Italian stallion.

Then he released her, and a cock shoved into her pussy.

"*Mio amore*," Landon groaned. "Your cunt is so tight around my cock."

The hands on her legs released her. She felt breathless and already another orgasm throbbed at her clit. A set of hands cradled her head and tilted it to the side.

"Open your mouth." It was Jake. His manhood pressed to her lips and she opened her mouth. He pushed inside and thrust his cock into her mouth, hitting the back of her throat.

Landon groaned out loud. His hair tickled her neck and his tongue swept over her neck. He bit into her neck and snarled next to her ear.

She groaned around the cock in her mouth and Jake pulled himself out.

"Over here, baby girl," Aidan said. She followed the sound of his voice and turned her head the other way. His hands cupped her head and his dick pressed against her lips. She opened her mouth and he pushed inside. "Oh hell, yes," he groaned.

Landon released her neck and licked the wound. "Time to share you, *mio amore.*" He pulled his cock from her pulsing core and slid his tongue over her nipples.

"Gods, her pussy. She's so fucking wet," Ethan groaned.

"I'm going to move," Jared whispered, and pulled himself out of her backside.

She nodded and lowered her legs to the floor. He pushed her up and held her body.

"Come here, beautiful angel," Ethan said and took her hands. She stood and he held onto her. "Do you need to rest a bit?"

"Hell, no. Give me your blood," she said with a pant.

He chuckled. "My pleasure." A second later, his arm was at her mouth. Lips peppered kisses along her back down to her ass. Ethan's blood pooled in her mouth and she swallowed with greed. Her energy lifted and her body ignited, ready for more.

She released his arm and ran her tongue over her mouth. "Who's next?"

"Bring her over here." She heard Jake behind her across the room.

"I have you," Ethan told her and took her by the arm. He led her across the room until a set of hands touched her thighs.

"Straddle my body, baby," Jake said and feathered his lips across her stomach. "No arms on this chair."

She nodded and held her hands out. He took them and pulled her forward. She placed her hands on his shoulders, then straddled him. He pressed his cock to her sex and pushed inside.

"Oh, fuck, yes," he groaned. "Damn, you feel good, baby."

She moved her hands to his face and touched his lips with her fingertips, then leaned forward. Her mouth slanted over his and she swiped her tongue inside his mouth.

Warm liquid slipped down the crack of her ass again.

"I'm behind you, baby," Ethan said. She bent down toward Jake and pushed her ass out, welcoming him. He pressed the head of his cock to her asshole and pushed in, easily breaching the thick ring of muscle.

She felt Ethan grip her hips and his body slapped against her ass. "Aidan," he called. "Come over here, brother. Come fuck this ass."

"My pleasure, my brother," Aidan told him.

A finger pushed between her lips. She sucked on it, not sure whose it was.

"So fucking hot," Jared whispered.

She circled her tongue around his finger and nibbled the end of it, then moved it from her mouth.

Ethan pulled free from her backside and some liquid slipped over her ass.

Another cock pushed into her channel and he thrust against her body.

"Damn, baby girl," Aidan groaned. "Fucking, yes!"

"*La mia amante, bella donna,*" Landon growled in her ear and wrapped his hand around her chin. He tilted her head to the side and pressed his lips to hers.

She gasped against his lips as another orgasm pulsated through her core. A growl rumbled in her chest and she threw her head back. "Holy fuck, holy fuck, holy fuck!"

Jake pulled free from her pussy and pushed his hand between them. His finger pressed against her clit and he moved it fast, side to side.

Ethan drove his cock faster into her ass.

Her hips bucked and she keened, long and low as the tide rushed in and another monstrous wave began to build before erupting in a wash of heat and descending over her.

"Yes! Fuck me, yes!" she screamed.

"My hand is fucking drenched. I love it," Jake whispered to her.

Ethan slowed down and then carefully pulled himself free.

Olivia leaned forward on Jake and pressed her forehead to his shoulder. "Holy hell, y'all, I need a minute. Please."

"You definitely earned more than a minute," Jared said. "I'm going to remove your blindfold, okay?"

She nodded and sat up in Jake's lap. The material around her head was untied and lowered. Switching from darkness to light was unforgiving at first, but after a moment, she was able to open her eyes.

She met Jake's gaze first. He winked at her and she grinned.

"Well, hello there, baby," Jake whispered. He trailed a fingertip over her cheek.

"Help me stand?" she asked.

"Let me pick you up. You've been through a lot just now," Jared told her.

She did not want to argue and honestly, she didn't think she could stand. She turned to him and moved herself from Jake and Jared scooped her up in his arms. She laid her head on his shoulder and let herself go.

"Will it be like this every day?" she asked.

"If you would like, yes, we can do this every day," he told her.

He began to walk and she wound her arms around his neck. Soon, the outdoor breeze surrounded her naked body and she shivered, but it wasn't necessarily cold. It was the realization this was her life.

Love filled her, completely.

Jared stepped into the hot tub and lowered her down. She remained in his lap and held onto him as the others stepped in with her. She met the gaze of each of her men, her stable, her life.

"I love you. Each of you," she told them.

"I love you," Jake announced first. She met his stare.

"I love you," Ethan and Aidan announced together.

"*Ti amo*," Landon said behind her and pressed his lips to her cheek.

She felt complete. She needed nothing, wanted for nothing, and had everything.

Tawne crossed her mind.

"Jared?"

"Yes, my love?"

She slipped off his lap and sat between him and Landon. "My friend Tawne. I want to bring her here. I want to spend time with her and meet y'all."

"Then, we'll make it happen," he told her.

She beamed with a nod. "Is there someone, or someone's, we may be able to introduce her to?"

He chuckled. "I don't run a dating service."

She blushed. "I know, and let me know if I'm overstepping, but if there's a chance, any chance at all for happiness for her in this world, she deserves it." She examined her hands under the water, twisting and twining the digits together as she spoke. "She was there for me when my mother wasn't."

Jared tilted her head up and feathered a kiss over her forehead. "Anything for you, my love. Consider it done."

She lifted her arms around his neck. She squeezed him close and inhaled his familiar scent. "Thank you, my Jared. Thank you."

She sat back and relaxed in the water. Olivia had a bad habit of getting caught up in her own head, causing insecurities. She bit her lip and frowned.

"What is it, my love," Jake asked her.

She sighed and shook her head. "It's stupid. Never mind."

"Nothing is stupid," Landon told her. "Tell us, what is it?"

She lifted her head and regarded to each of her men. "What happens when I age and grow old?"

"We'll worry about that later," Jared told her.

"Besides, you have a lifetime with us. Why worry about that?" Ethan asked.

"Because, eventually, it'll happen."

"Not if there's a way to keep you young," Jared told her.

Her eyes widened, and she turned her attention to him. "What?"

"There may be a way. We'll discuss it with the elders when your friend, Tawne, is presented for pairing."

She hugged him again. "Thank you so much. I do love you, each of you, so much."

Olivia was born a blood demon, destined to serve the vampire community. What was once fear for the unknown became the most amazing, beautiful, love-filled life she ever could have imagined. Love, hope, and fulfillment consumed her completely. She could not have asked for a happier ending.

THE END

If you enjoyed The Concubine and Her Vampires, please consider leaving a review. Even a few words can make an Author's day so much brighter.

Turn the page for a taste from The Human and Her Vampires, Book Two in the Covenant of New Orleans series.

Excerpt

The Human and Her Vampires

Can dreams become reality...

Tawne O'Brien loves adventure and dreams of living in a world where paranormal creatures exist. Orphaned at a young age, and with a string of failed relationships only adding to her misery, her books are the only salvation from a mundane existence in a universe where she feels completely alone. When her best friend asks her to come visit, her dreams of a new life suddenly become a possibility.

Tawne is introduced to four sexy-as-sin vampires and given the opportunity of a lifetime with no strings attached...or so they say. When she discovers she may only be a guinea pig to the vampires, disappointment regains the upper hand, reminding her of her place in this world.

Can Tawne find the strength inside herself to fight for what she deserves?

If she doesn't, she'll lose everything...including any memory of her life with her vampires.

Chapter One

A CRISP BREEZE weaved its way through the streets below the indigo sky of New Orleans, Louisiana. The night was clear and the stars flickered in the heavens, as if teasing one another with the mere wink of an eye. The full moon bright as it cast its path along the trees to form unusual shadows on the ground.

It was just before dawn and in the distance of the eastern horizon, the dawn of a new day began.

Tourists would pack the streets tonight. They would drink their beers, chase one another to see who would end up with the most beads, then head out on a walking tour of vampires in Downtown New Orleans.

And they say it was all just a myth, a part of the city's charm. Although, some days, Tawne O'Brien had hoped for more. She loved the paranormal romance books she read. From being swept up by a star-crossed lover, to finding her soul mate after many reincarnations... But, alas, it was only fiction.

Summer had come to an end around late October. Halloween would be here soon. It was one of Tawne's favorite holidays. Maybe this year she'd dress up as a witch, or a fairy. Maybe a vampire.

She stood out on her deck of her condo on the second floor. The wind blew a gentle breeze around her body. Long tendrils of blonde hair drifted around her shoulders.

Tawne's phone chimed a new text message and vibrated in her pocket. She reached inside and pulled her phone out. A text from Matthew: her current, but soon to be ex, boyfriend. She sighed and rolled her eyes. She'd known early on, during the budding of their relationship, Matthew wasn't the one. He was nice, and one day would make someone happy, but not her.

I want to see you later, the text read.

She had put this off long enough. There was a wall, at least five feet thick, between them, theoretically speaking. She hit reply and began a text.

Listen, we need to talk.

She shook her head, erased the letters on the screen, then tried again.

I think we need to call it quits.

She erased that and tried once more.

Matthew, look, I can't do this anymore. You're great and all, but it's me, not you. I'm not happy. I need to figure out what I need for me, before I can give myself to someone else. I hope you understand.

She hit send. As soon as it was sent, she turned off her phone. He would probably call her, demand an answer, try to talk her out of it, or hell, come over.

She stepped back inside her condo and closed the sliding door behind her. White walls surrounded her with artwork from the local design stores. She crossed the room to her study where her laptop rested open at her wooden corner desk. She sat down and pressed a few keys until the screen flickered out of sleep mode.

The background image displayed Tawne with her parents. An ache in her chest thumped with the beat of her heart. Having died young in an accident not of their own doing took them from her too soon. Her heart ached for a hug from her father, or a kiss on her cheek from her mother. She swiped at a tear that wet her cheek.

Shaking off the sadness, she clicked on the message app. She wanted to send a note over to Olivia, her best friend. They had fallen out of touch with one another. This would be a great time to pick up their friendship.

Olivia had pushed her out of her life when her mother passed away. She knew her friend needed space and time to heal but had not counted on it taking more than a few months.

How long has it been since we talked? A year? Maybe two? Some best friend I am. I've been so self-obsessed with finding someone to date... I'm a bitch.

She began a message to Olivia and started it with, "Well, I'm a seriously nasty bitch. And I love you," when the video app on her computer turned on without warning.

Fuck, don't let it be Matthew. Don't let it be Matthew.

Tawne smiled when she saw Olivia's name flash across the screen. She pressed accept. Olivia's face came into view and Tawne gasped.

"Tawne!" Olivia squealed. "Ohmigawd, it has been too long! Look at you! I love your hair! It's so long!"

Tawne blinked, then chuckled. "Well, I was just starting a message to you, and here you are. Wow, look at you! Whatever you're doing, it's good for you. I haven't seen you look this good, this happy, this... I don't know, glowing? Ever!"

Olivia grinned, and then let out a giggle. A crimson flush crept up her cheeks as she cast her gaze downward.

Tawne lifted a brow. "Okay, spill, who are you seeing and what the hell have you been up to?"

Olivia lifted her gaze back to the monitor and her demeanor calmed. "That's kinda why I was calling. Do you think we could meet up?"

Tawne grinned. "Of course! I'd love to see you. You're my best friend. Tell me when and where."

Her friend nibbled on her finger, then turned to someone talking to her in the distance. Tawne heard a man's voice.

She grinned. "So, who's the mister in the background?"

Olivia turned back to the camera and gave a grin so sly it could melt ice. "We'll talk about that, too. I'm going to message you an address. I'll be there waiting for you."

"This is kinda mysterious," Tawne teased her. "Have you gone into hiding or something?"

Olivia shrugged. "Or something."

The smile on Tawne's lips fell to a frown. "Are you okay?"

"Oh yes! I'm beyond okay. I'm absolutely amazing! My life... Oh, Tawne, I cannot wait to tell you all about it. Just not over the phone, okay?"

Tawne nodded. She wondered if she should go prepared for a fight. She'd heard of men controlling their women and not allowing them to have friends. If this was Olivia's case, she would whip out her bat and her krav maga moves. She had no shame in taking down a man. She would do it if it meant helping out a female in a bad situation.

"All right," Tawne said and sat back in her chair. "I'll see you soon, then. I cannot wait to hug you!"

"Yes!" Olivia squealed again. "I'll see you soon! Muah!" She blew an air kiss into the camera, then the screen went black.

Tawne had always been the quirky one. Feeling awkward in most situations, she became an introverted extrovert. She was quiet until she got to know you. She found herself smiling more often when she was alone in her own thoughts. In her friendship with Olivia, though, it was Olivia who was down more often than not. It's not that she was a Debbie Downer, but more like she lived a life of depression. It was who she was, and Olivia accepted that about herself. She was alone in the world...just like Tawne. Except for each other, they didn't have anyone else in the world.

Olivia often told her she was the sunshine to the dark storm of her life. As Olivia's best friend, Tawne was there when Olivia lost her mother, and helped her deal with the fall out afterward.

When Olivia left town shortly after, she'd told Tawne that she had to go overseas for some family ceremony. It appeared the family issues were over, and she was back home.

Olivia said she would text the address. For now, that was good enough. She didn't want to turn the phone back on in case Matthew tried calling. She didn't want to deal with voice mails or questions from him. She needed a night out on her own. New movies were at the theater and there was a new action flick staring this hot, up and coming actor.

Tawne grabbed her purse and walked to the bathroom. Facing her reflection in the mirror, she picked up her lip-gloss off the counter. She slid a dab of the light pink gloss over her lips, then tucked the tube into her purse. Satisfied with how she looked, she slipped on her sandals and headed to her front door.

Tonight, would be movie night on her own, with her thoughts. She was ready to find herself. In order to do that, it meant finding happiness as well. She knew that to make it in a relationship, she would have to bring something to the table other than lust and false pretenses of a future she knew she could not provide.

Her parents taught her never to sell herself short and never settle for less than what she deserved. They often reminded her of this, but the last time they did, she'd waved them off with a flick of her hand. If she had known that would be the last time she would see them, talk to them, hug them, she would have taken the time to hug and kiss their cheeks, and tell them how much she loved them.

Olivia was there for her during her emotional outbursts. She'd returned the favor when Olivia had lost her mother.

Tawne pushed the reminiscent thoughts from her mind, closed her apartment door behind her and clicked the thick deadbolt lock into place. Tonight, would be the movies. Tomorrow she'd meet up with Olivia and figure out what she'd been doing overseas, and what the plans were now.

Find Book Two in the Covenant of New Orleans series, The Human and Her Vampires now on Amazon.

Other Books by Julie Morgan

1. FALLEN

2. REDEMPTION

3. ATONEMENT

4. CULMINATION

STAND ALONE STORIES

DRAGON MASTER

STONE OBSESSION

DEADLY ALCHEMY SERIES

1. DEADLY ALCHEMY

DEADLY ALCHEMY (on audio)

2. FATAL ALCHEMY

3. WICKED ALCHEMY

THE SYMPHONY SERIES

1. SYMPHONY OF NIGHT

2. SYMPHONY OF POWER

3. SYMPHONY OF FATE

About the Author

USA TODAY BESTSELLING and Award-winning Author, Julie Morgan, holds a degree in Computer Science and loves science fiction shows and movies. Encouraged by her family, she began writing.

Originally from Texas, Julie now resides in Central Florida with her husband and daughter where she is an advocate for Special Needs children and can be found playing games with her daughter when she isn't lost in another world.

For more information please visit her at

www.juliemorganbooks.com

Facebook:

https://www.facebook.com/juliemorganbook

Twitter: @juliemorganbook

Web site and blog:

www.juliemorganbooks.com